*The Twelve Stories of Christmas*

Order this book online at www.trafford.com
or email orders@trafford.com

Most Trafford titles are also available at major online book retailers.

Print information available on the last page.

ISBN: 978-1-4120-8227-3 (sc)
ISBN: 978-1-4122-0220-6 (hc)
ISBN: 978-1-4251-9431-4 (e)

*Trafford rev. 10/29/2018*

**North America & international**
toll-free: 1 888 232 4444 (USA & Canada)
fax: 812 355 4082

# The Twelve Stories of Christmas

By

## DR. JERRY DICKEY

Illustrated by

*Patsy Ashley Given*

These stories are fiction. Except for a few details regarding the author's life, all of the incidents, names, and characters are imaginary.

"O Holy Night:" Story Eight
"O Holy Night" is of French origin. Adolphe Charles Adam (1856), wrote the tune to a poem (Cantique de Noel) by M. Cappeau de Roquemaure. The English translation was made by John Sullivan Dwight (1893).

To

BARRY LEE KEIDEL,
a true friend for half my lifetime,
and his wife KIM

They provided the place to work
and the peace of mind to write.

# *Preface*

Wherever, whenever darkness surrounds human life,
the light of hope shines ever brighter.

J. D.

April 2006

# Contents

# *Acknowledgments*

Needless to say, from a book that emerges over a 40-year span of time, many groups and individuals have assisted in bringing these Christmas stories to life.

Little did I know that two persons whose families received a Christmas letter in 1965 would, in 2005, become editors for my works and prepare these stories for this book. Deborah Randall Cornelius and Stephanie Emory Gradinger have capably and lovingly edited these writings into this storybook format from pages of print in the form of stories comprised of long paragraphs with some very long sentences. Like workers who carefully and painstakingly scrape thin layers of earth from an artifact dig, they kept my thoughts and personal touches intact. Deborah and Stephanie were in "The Lamplighters" singing group I directed from 1965 to 1967 which toured to Boston, New York City, and Washington D.C. Together they have kept the music in my writings for this book alive.

That first attempt of story writing, in the form of a Christmas letter sent to friends and family, became the predecessor of "The Twelve Stories of Christmas" which I wrote from 1973 to 2003. Over the years, those stories were read to hundreds of persons in churches during Advent/Christmas seasons.

The artwork of Patsy Ashley Given throughout the pages of this book, as well as on the front and back cover, is that of a long-time, very dear friend.

Living and traveling across the country and around the globe has given me an appreciation for different perspectives and ways of living that 'light up' these stories. My undergraduate work in Delaware, Ohio, master's degree in Boston, Massachusetts, and doctorate in Berkeley, California surrounded me with friends and intellectual growth. Studies in Denmark, Germany, and France provided an even wider perspective. Those influences can be seen throughout this book.

Others I wish to acknowledge are:

Rev. Jerry K. Hill, who created sets, designed lighting, and encouraged the writing and presentation of the last six stories of this book.

Dr. Paul D. Tropf, who encouraged me to get a doctorate in the creative arts, and who has been a friend for 30 years.

Betty Moon and Susie Griffith, two secretaries who made possible the Christmas letter in 1965, and who started me on this writing journey.

Steve and Kathy Conner, who provided a quiet, upstairs retreat for me to write several of these stories, and a grand piano to compose music to enhance several of them.

Rick and Susie Conrad, who helped me create a

story, fill out forms, and read and re-read edited copies of stories.

My thanks to the Cann family, especially Dr. Will Cann, who hosted me in Europe, and took the trip with me back to Denmark before completing "Christmas Far From Home."

Thanks also to the Ahrens family, and notably Andy, who made an impossibly difficult snowy trip home from school to sing and participate in the performance of my last story.

And, a special thanks to the extended Dickey and Seese families who have blessed my life.

Finally, I am deeply appreciative for the heartfelt response of the people and colleagues at Cochituate, Glenwood, Central, Armstrong, First, and Clifton. Their joy, hugs, tears, and smiles made it all worthwhile.

Dr. Jerry Dickey
July 16, 2006

# *Opening Letters*

Dear Jerry,

***Here are my thoughts to those who open the pages of this book:***

Our paths through life twist and turn and are sometimes poorly lit. If you've had the good fortune to meet my friend Jerry, then you will surely have seen his light and felt the warmth of its glow. I first saw it in a snowy medieval town in Germany a long time ago. It lit up the faces of the townsfolk who paused on the frozen cobblestones to huddle and listen as Jerry and his impromptu choir filled the town square with joyous song. Christmas 1967 was a milestone in the lives of young men and women from all corners of the earth whose paths crossed with Jerry's in that ancient Bavarian town far from home.

Jerry's road shares our ups and downs, but he has always held his light up high for those who inhabit his world. It shines beyond creed and culture. It's the light of love, of caring and giving. And his message is one of faith and hope.

Get ready to meet Jerry as you read through his collection of Christmas stories. May the glow of his beacon warm your heart and light your way, too.

Blessings from Japan.

Dein Zwilling,

Rick Brueggemann
Kobe, Japan

My dear good friend Jerry!

It is a great honor and pleasure to be asked by you to write some words for your new book. It is more than 37 years ago, when we met for the first time in March of 1968 at the "International House of Sonnenberg" in northern Germany for a week's study course. I had no idea then, that from this first meeting, it would develop into a wonderful friendship lasting a lifetime. I remember your visits in the home of my parents, and although they didn't speak English, they understood your growing German vocabulary. Through the years, you were always welcome.

I was very excited, in May 1972, to go with you to the USA, to visit your homeland, and to live with your family in Ohio, as you had done with mine.

Dear Jerry, do you remember our sightseeing tour of New York City, our trips to Columbus and Cleveland, and especially our visit to the River Front Stadium in Cincinnati, where I saw my first baseball game?

All this was a really great experience for me. And I thank you for taking me under your wing, and for all the kindnesses of your family and friends.

Through the years, my wife Barbara, our children, and my sister Uschi and her family have enjoyed your return visits.

I am proud to have a friend like you, and I am happy that through this book, more and more people can enjoy these stories created throughout your life's journey! "Alles gute!"

Your German brother,

Helmut Dudel
Immensen, Germany

Dear Jerry,

Greetings to your readers from Denmark!

Jerry's story called "Christmas Far From Home" is about one of the Christmases he celebrated with my family in Denmark. This particular Christmas of 1967 has a special meaning for both Jerry and me, and for our relationship today. I was born only 10 days before Jerry arrived at our home for Christmas on December 23rd, the very day I was brought home from the hospital.

Jerry has always been part of my family – kind of an "uncle from America." He met my father, Poul Erik Thomsen, at the Ollerup Gymnastic College in Denmark, in July of 1967. By then I was four months along in my mother's pregnancy. Jerry often mentions Aalborg, Denmark, where we lived, as his "home away from home." Though I naturally do not remember that first Christmas of mine in 1967, I have many memories of Jerry's later visits and holidays in Aalborg with my parents and my younger brothers, Jeppe and Jakob. My husband, Jakob Lindahl, and I have had the privilege of getting a visit from Jerry in our present home in Copenhagen, and we hope to get more, so that our young kids, Valdemar and Katinka, get to meet the uncle from America that I tell so many stories about. I hope you will enjoy the story about this particular Christmas of 1967!

Lotte Thomsen
M.A. Economic Geography
PhD Researcher

# A Christmas Letter

# CHRISTMAS

Christmas! The word fascinated the nine-year-old boy as he pressed his nose against the department store window. The icy cold pane made his nose turn red except the tiny spot that was tightly pressed against the window. "It was worth it, though," he thought to himself. He just wanted to get a closer look at the animated happiness taking place inside the store. Above the toyland scene one word was written in large red letters – CHRISTMAS – and around it hung dazzling white snowflakes trimmed with silver glitter. Christmas – the boy's head slowly came away from the windowpane and his smiling face grew thoughtful.

Christmas held so many different meanings for the people he knew. Grandma and Grandpa flashed into his mind first. They were always there on Christmas Day, but Christmas wasn't for them somehow. "They seem to enjoy me and my Christmas more than their own," he thought to himself.

Suddenly, a tumbling giant package struck him on the elbow and sent him sprawling to the ground. For one moment he looked as if he were part of the display on the inside of the window instead of an outside observer. The man turned as the boy was getting up, brushing his jacket with his glove. "I'm sorry kid," came the quick, deep-toned apology. The boy heard the man mumble to his wife, as they walked away, "I wonder why parents don't keep track of their kids."

"Parents," he thought to himself, "It's hard to tell if they really enjoy Christmas. They're so busy getting ready! What was the word used in Sunday School? 'Preparation.' " The teacher had spent the whole morning telling them about preparation.

The boy pulled his red scarf up tighter around his neck. A sound of screeching tires forced him to turn in time to see a big blue car send a little red one spinning in a circle to the tune of tinkling glass. The crowd stopped and gathered at the curb a few feet in front of the boy and his animated window. Traffic jammed, horns honked, and soon a siren was heard off in the distance. Above the noise he heard a girl say, "I don't think anyone's hurt badly, but you can't tell."

And a man's bitter voice spoke out: "The law of averages is bound to get you sooner or later."

"Preparation." The big word stuck in the boy's mind. "Whatever do you suppose we're getting ready for?"

The boy turned almost as if he expected the elves and dolls to have disappeared, but there they were as active as ever, still smiling. The presents in the brightly colored windows were beautifully wrapped, especially the one from which the puppy dog kept popping.

"Presents. The teacher said Sunday that our presents should help say it is Christ's birthday." The boy thought for a moment. "Now what would best say it is Christ's birthday?"

He thought over the familiar Christmas stories in

4

the Bible and soon made his decision. An angel. Not a singing one, because he had too hard a time singing in tune. He decided on an angel with a trumpet. Now he had to find enough for his entire family.

"Let's see. Mother, Dad, Grandma and Grandpa (that could be one to save money), and my little brother. That's four."

A quick glance at the big clock outside the city bank told him he'd have to do some quick shopping, in order to be on time to meet his parents.

He walked into the store and the first thing that caught his eye was a gold pin on the jewelry counter. It was an angel with a long trumpet. He walked to the counter and standing on his toes to look taller, he began in his deepest tenor voice. "I'd like to buy one of those," he said to the lady in the blue frock as he pointed to the angel pin.

"That's three dollars, honey, plus tax."

The boy slowly melted from his tiptoes to his natural height.

"Oh," came the soft reply. "I only have four dollars," he sighed, almost talking to himself, "and I want to get four presents."

"Why don't you try the store next door, honey," she replied. "They have some cheaper things there." She turned to a tall lady in a red coat and a pink hat. "What can I do for you, honey?"

He walked past the animated window as the cold wind whistled and wound his black hair in twists above his head. His hands were in his pockets and his gaze was directed at his feet on the neatly ordered blocks of concrete sidewalk. His ears caught the sound of trumpets in a small band and at the same time he saw a foot tapping under a black dress. As though she expected him, he turned to the woman on the bench and blurted out, "Do you know what I'm going to do when I grow up?"

The woman accepted the statement like his father accepted his morning coffee, so the boy felt at ease to continue.

"I'm going to build a store where anyone can come in at Christmas and get anything he wants for however much he wants to pay!"

The woman's smile reminded him of Mary Poppins as she put her tambourine on her lap and folded her hands over the scattered nickels and dimes.

"And however will you do that?" she said with all seriousness. Her high voice was as clear as the church bells chiming above the frosty air.

It's almost angelic thought the boy as he continued. "Oh, I probably won't be able to build one, but we surely need a store like that. I've got four dollars to buy four angels with trumpets."

"Why do you want angels?" she questioned.

"Well, in Sun...do you go to Sunday School?"

The woman smiled from within. "I teach Sunday School," she replied.

"Then you should understand," the boy said with a sigh of relief. "Our teacher told us Sunday that our presents should help tell it is Christ's birthday," he continued, "and since angels told the shepherds about Jesus so many years ago, I just thought they would help tell us again today."

There was a quiet silence as the boy looked into the woman's face. Her blue eyes were warm and assuring, and still they revealed a depth that seemed to scan the centuries.

"I think I can help you," she said with a smile.

The boy sat beside her as she reached into the right pocket of her black coat. Out came a handful of small white cards. She handed one to the boy to read. There were four angels with trumpets around a scroll with words that read: "FOR UNTO YOU IS BORN THIS DAY IN THE CITY OF DAVID A SAVIOUR, WHICH IS CHRIST THE LORD" (Luke 2:11 KJV). The woman reached in another pocket and pulled out tiny envelopes for the cards. On the front was a silver angel with a long gold trumpet and a space where a name could be written.

"How much are they?" the boy quickly asked.

"You may have as many as you wish. There is no cost."

"But I have four dollars..."

"The best presents you can give at Christmas are those that cost you nothing. After all, God gave the greatest present and neither you nor I have to pay for it."

She noticed the boy was still uneasy for he had come to town to buy something.

"I'll tell you what you can buy," she said as she lifted the tambourine. "Every quarter you give helps some boy or girl or man or woman have a Merry Christmas that otherwise would have none."

The boy reached into his little pocket and unfolded two dollar bills. He folded them carefully again and put them in an envelope and on the front he printed: MERRY CHRISTMAS TO EVERYONE. He put the envelope in the tambourine.

"If you give me five of the cards then Grandma and Grandpa can each have one," he said with a glow in his eyes.

She handed five cards and envelopes to him as a man in a black suit came to take her place. The woman picked up her trumpet and waved goodbye to the boy as she walked toward the small band of players. The boy waved and went hurrying down the street. The clock said he was five minutes late, but he wasn't worried. He felt a greater happiness within than he had felt at any other Christmas. As he turned the corner, he saw his mother and father in front of the animated window.

"I have my presents," he said as he felt the edges of the cards in his pocket. "And I talked with an angel in black."

His father glanced at his mother with a wrinkled brow.

"A what?" asked his father.

"But angels wear white, Gary," added his mother.

"I know," he said with a smile, "but some don't."

*December 1965*
*© Dr. Jerry Dickey*

# The Twelve Stories of Christmas

# THE RAGAMUFFIN

*Story One*

*The night that the baby Jesus was born was one of the most significant events in the entire world. Through the generations, we focus on that event, and hope connects the past with the present and the future. So, a tale is born connecting the birth of Christ with humble gifts from the ages.*

Quite a few people were squeezed into the tiny town of Bethlehem, and many of them were strangers. Some were children who heard, by way of a young shepherd boy, of a new baby that God had given to the world one very lonely night. The shepherd boy's news spread from child to child until it reached every corner of the earth. With love and goodwill in their hearts, these children began to gather gifts from their homes in far away lands. They set off with friends to greet the baby Jesus.

Children came from every corner of the world. Down from the mountains they came. From palm covered valleys and across snow covered plains they came ... from rainforests, and desert sands and jungles and grassy fields. They rode their favorite animals from their homelands. As they met new friends they found their way to travel toward Bethlehem. Like any journey, it wasn't always easy, and there were problems to overcome on the way. Yet, they continued until they reached the tiny town of Bethlehem.

It was an exciting time as the children began to

gather in Bethlehem. They wished their parents back home could have been with them because so many older people had forgotten how to be excited about living. Many of the people the children had left behind were too concerned about how they were going to die. These children were concerned with how they were going to live, and how they were going to give something to their emerging world. Most importantly, they wanted to find the new baby that God had sent for them to love, and give him the special gifts they brought from home.

They had heard that they were to look for a stable — a small grey barn behind the little hotel in the town — where the baby and his parents were living. Somehow it didn't seem like the best place for a little baby to stay, but then the children had come to make his beginnings more pleasant anyway.

By the time they arrived in Bethlehem, the children were tired. As they met on the edge of town, a dirty Ragamuffin jumped into their midst. Whether it was the hour of the evening or the startled movement of his appearance that sent them scurrying, we'll never know, but quicker than a twinkling star, the curious little boy was all alone in the city street. He could hardly believe his eyes because he only wanted to find out what was happening and to be included. He certainly didn't wish to be left alone. He had enough of being left alone as it was.

The little Ragamuffin kicked a stone down the dusty street, as starlight caught the flurry of foreign clothing scattering in the still night air. He was disappointed, no doubt about it. It was apparent in the way he walked.

He probably would have returned to the dark corner of his favorite side street, if he hadn't seen the movement of a child in the distance. He noticed her going back and forth as if she were hunting for something. He made no startling move, but with a quizzical look that could only be read as real concern, he approached the little girl.

"Excuse me," the Ragamuffin said with caution, "but can I help?"

"Oh," the girl sighed, "I lost the things I brought in my wooden shoe for the Christ child. Now I have no berries, nuts, and evergreen to fill it. All I have left is a big wooden shoe. I wish I could have lost the shoe instead of the things in it! What will I do now?"

"Don't worry," he said, "I can help!"

Off they went down the street. He knew where to find berry branches, and on the way they found the evergreen branch Maria-Louise had dropped when she came into town. He hurried into the marketplace, which hadn't yet closed. He paid the man two of the little coins he had been saving, and placed some nuts in the shoe. Maria-Louise rubbed the soot off one of his cheeks, and gave the Ragamuffin a pat on the shoulder before skipping off down the dark street.

Scarcely had he turned around when he spotted another girl sitting sadly at the side of the road on a large, heavy coat. Her name was Inka.

"What's the matter?" he inquired.

"I've lost my gift," she said, "I've lost my necklace! My father carved it from whalebone. I know I had it in my pocket at the town gate, but now it's gone. It's gone!"

17

"Have you looked for it?" he asked.

"A little, but I'm so tired, and it's beginning to get dark, and I don't know the town."

"Well, which way did you come into town?" questioned the Ragamuffin.

She pointed down the street to the right.

"Stay here, I know the town well." And off he went in the dark.

A bright light from a star shone over the town that night, so a white necklace was easy for the boy to find. He returned to Inka, and was rewarded by seeing the warmth return to her face and eyes to match the warm coat on which she was sitting.

"I think it will make a nice present for the Christ child," she smiled.

"For the Christ child?" he questioned.

"Yes," she returned.

"Who is the Christ child?" asked the Ragamuffin.

"He is God's gift to everyone, we've heard, and to children everywhere for all future years,"

"For...for me too?" the Ragamuffin asked hesitantly.

"For everyone, we've heard," she said happily. She smiled and as she turned she almost bumped into a boy pacing back and forth.

Klaus was examining a lantern with a discouraged frown.

"Why so unhappy?" inquired the Ragamuffin.

"The light in my lantern is out," returned the boy sadly, "and since I'm a stranger in town, I have no fire to re-light it." It was a real problem, for what's a beautiful homemade lantern with no light to make it glow?

"Come with me," said the Ragamuffin, as he motioned the boy toward a house. "There's a family I know that's always helping others," he said as they continued down the street. "If ever I don't have food to eat, they always have some to share so that I don't have to go hungry. They're as dependable as the shepherds on the hillsides," assured the Ragamuffin.

No sooner had they knocked on the door than the light was given. The lantern now glowed like the bright star over Bethlehem as the boy wound his way down the street.

As the Ragamuffin turned from Klaus, he noticed a solitary figure in a white turban sitting dejected, staring off into the night. The Ragamuffin didn't say a word. He just sat down quietly next to the boy and waited for him to speak.

"The answer lies within someone else," the boy with the white turban began.

"I beg your pardon?" replied the Ragamuffin.

The boy, Govindaiha, spoke slowly, "At home, I have been taught when I have a problem, to sit and quietly reflect until I have an answer."

"And do you have an answer?" the Ragamuffin questioned.

"Yes," said the dark eyed boy quietly, "the answer is, someone else has to find the answer for me. I brought a gift of incense for the baby Jesus. I wanted to start it burning before I went to the stable."

"I have an answer," smiled the Ragamuffin. "A new friend of mine has a light in his lantern – he can't be far down the street. Follow me."

Off they went. They didn't even have to turn the corner before they saw the glow of the lantern ahead of them. The incense lent a pleasing smell to the night air, and one couldn't begin to find happier children anywhere than those who began to emerge in the little town of Bethlehem.

Tired from all his running about, the Ragamuffin found a place to sit. "God's gift," he thought to himself, "to children everywhere for all future years." He had never heard of a gift that lasted forever. No wonder the children were excited about giving the baby something in return.

Before he could remind himself that other than the two coins left in his pocket, there was nothing in the world for him to give, a boy almost ran into him as he darted about in a frantic search. The Ragamuffin had a hard time catching up with him, and a harder time getting him to stand in one place long enough to tell what he lost.

It was a pinata full of toys that looked like a rooster! Paco had it with him when he arrived, but now it was gone. The Ragamuffin knew it was too big to be lost along the street somewhere without someone seeing it, so he thought someone must have taken it home until the owner was found. It might take some time, but he decided to take the boy with him, door to door, and ask politely if the rooster had been found. After three tries with no luck, at the fourth house a lady told them of a family who spread the news that they had found it. They had it at their home in safe keeping for the owner. When the gift had been returned and the boy was calm, the Ragamuffin asked him why all the children came to Bethlehem to look for the child. Why not another town? Paco told him that the bright new star led them to Bethlehem, and suggested that he go to the edge of the village to see it for himself.

The Ragamuffin arrived at the edge of the village where there was a solitary figure standing by a wall.

"Have you lost something too?"

The girl bowed, and then shook her head no. She told him that she had brought rice candy for the Christ child, which was in a beautiful gleaming white dish. But now the candy was in a rough piece of cloth, for the dish had broken when she dropped it crossing the mountains on her way to Bethlehem. He almost suggested that the dish wasn't important, but when she mentioned that she had helped to paint it, he tried only to think of a way to help. Then he remembered that behind the potter's shop every day they threw away things that they couldn't use. He took the little girl by the hand, and off they went to the potter's shop. The little girl had a brush with her, which she used to paint things she saw on her journey – presents to take home to her family. They searched the pile of leftover pottery, and finally found a perfectly good piece that the little girl thought, with a little work, would look very nearly like her own. They mixed some powder into paint from a chalky stone pile nearby. The Ragamuffin held the dish while she painted, and at last the project was finished. The two were amazed at its simple beauty.

As the girl bowed to leave, a young boy brushed by the Ragamuffin. At first, he thought it was Klaus pacing once again, but upon closer look, he saw another boy.

"Did you break your gift or lose it?" the Ragamuffin began with confidence.

Aleksei gave him a double glance and quickly responded, "Neither. I gave it away. On my way to Bethlehem, I met many people, but there were three in particular who happily helped me find my way: an old woman, a boy working in a field, and a poor little child outside the gate of an old village. None of them had any food. They could not have lived without bread, so I gave my bread to them. For how could I be happy here if I knew I had left people behind in sadness? So I was pacing up and down these steps trying to figure out what I could use to replace the gift I had given away."

"Why not replace bread with bread!" the Ragamuffin said with a gleam in his eye as he motioned for the boy to follow. They arrived at the baker's shop huffing and puffing, but the windows were already dark. The Ragamuffin gave a knock on the door, and soon there was a light and the door opened a crack. His last two coins were exchanged for a loaf of bread, and once again someone had been helped.

Somehow the Ragamuffin had forgotten all about the bread he was counting on for supper. As he walked out under the starlit night, he felt the warmth of the light from the big star that Paco had told him about, and found he wasn't even hungry.

"A gift for all children forever," he thought to himself. He stood quietly in the silence for five minutes, maybe more. Then the Ragamuffin noticed a light moving toward him. As the ebony-faced boy approached him, he was smiling. A small, hand-held Aladdin-like lamp flickered with its dancing light.

"That's a beautiful light," the Ragamuffin said.

"A Rabbi gave it to me in the last town," Samuel replied. "He told me hospitality toward a stranger was important, and since I only had one beeswax candle left from home, the Rabbi insisted that I take the lamp so I would have enough light to find my way."

Suddenly the two boys heard someone crying. They followed the sound of the voice, and discovered a girl quite overtaken by sobs and gentle tears.

"What is it? What is the matter?" they said softly so as not to startle her.

The voices seemed to bring her out of her sadness. She lifted a crown from her head and showed the two boys three candles where there should have been four. The tow-headed girl wiped her eyes, but before she could explain, the Ragamuffin and Samuel looked at each other, smiling. Samuel took his remaining beeswax candle, and slipped it into the crown.

"Now your gift is complete," Samuel said. "When one receives light, one can give light to others."

The Ragamuffin walked quietly down the street as though the candles were aglow within him. A beautiful bronze-skinned girl looking out the window of a house called out as the Ragamuffin passed by.

"Are you going to see the Christ child tonight?" she asked.

In all this busy night, it was the first time the question came to him. He shrugged his shoulders as an indication of his surprise and lack of thought on the subject. But then he spoke, "I don't have a present. Do you have a present?"

"Yes," she said, "right here," and she waved a palm branch she had brought from home.

"Well, then, you're the first one who hasn't lost or broken something along the way," he replied.

"I have my present, but I did forget something."

"What have you forgotten?" he asked.

"A red flower for my hair. I always wear one at home when I am to greet someone for the first time, and I just wish I had one to wear tonight."

"Wait a minute," said the Ragamuffin.

He fairly skipped down the street. "Friends," he thought to himself, "what an important part of life. So many strangers from all over the world are now my friends."

Right where he knew it would be, he picked a desert flower – brilliantly red.

"Friends," he thought as he presented the flower, "It takes so little to make the world smile again. It doesn't matter what you look like; it's only how you make others look that counts."

The Ragamuffin sat on a street corner as the children

of the world began to gather. The girl's question rang in his ears, "Are you going to see the Christ child tonight?" He felt his now empty pocket as children continued to gather. He knew his answer to her question now. It would have to be "no" because he had nothing to give. Unnoticed, he quietly crawled around the corner and into an alleyway where he would not be seen. Sitting there in the dark, he knew that even though he would not go, he would be present through the lives of all the other children as they took their gifts to the Christ child.

One by one as the children gathered, they began to talk about their gifts, and one by one they learned that none of them would have been there if it hadn't been for the dirty-faced, tattered and torn Ragamuffin. Then they noticed that he was no longer around.

"Where do you suppose he went?" questioned one.

"We can't go to see the Christ child without him," exclaimed another.

"After all, he's part of us. Without him, not one of us would be prepared to see the Christ child!"

The girls came up with a suggestion:

"Let's all spread out and cover the town and see if we can find him. We can meet back here in a few minutes." Off they went as quickly as they had scattered when they first had laid eyes on the Ragamuffin. They looked up and down the streets. They knocked on doors. They asked neighbors, and questioned strangers. They checked the home that gave the light, the bakery, and behind the pottery shed. Just as they were about to give up, they heard a call in the clear night air. It was the girl with the red flower in her hair. Quickly they gathered round to hear the news.

"He doesn't think he looks good enough to visit the new baby King," she told them.

"Then it's our turn to help him," cried Paco.

"Our turn to help him!" came the echoes down a dozen streets as children scattered across town. And help they did. Wool, needles, and thread were given. All of the children helped. It was so much fun that it was almost like a party. Soon the clothes were finished. The boys took the garment into the alley where the Ragamuffin had gone while the others anxiously waited. When he stepped out, the children could hardly believe their eyes.

"But I still don't have anything to give," the Ragamuffin said apologetically. The group turned to Govindaiha, for they knew he would search for the answer. "I think the best thing a person can give to the baby Jesus is just oneself," he said thoughtfully.

With that the children cheered, and the Ragamuffin smiled. "I'll show you the way to the stable behind the old hotel," he motioned.

*Century after century on that holy night, children of the world join together to make their way to the stable where the Christ-child is born.*

*December 24, 1973*
*© Dr. Jerry Dickey*

"Ragamuffin's New Clothes"

# THE SMALLEST SHEPHERD

## Story Two

It was nighttime on the hillside. An eleven-year-old boy sat on the stump of an olive tree overlooking the flickering lights of the lamps dotting windows below him in the small town of Bethlehem. The older shepherds slept on the ground behind him, and he was alone.

The words rang clearly in his mind. They had struck home sharply. "You are too small to be a shepherd, Aaron. You are a silly boy to think you can do the work of a man!"

It hadn't been the first time they had made fun of him. Aaron was small for his age, but he tried his best to keep up with the others. It had always been difficult, but since his father had died, he had missed the hand on his shoulder now and then letting him know that someone believed in him, even when the rest of the world did not. Aaron was so glad for the hours his father had spent with him each week studying the scriptures. And he looked forward to his trip to the temple in four short months when he would be twelve. Then he would be recognized by Israel as a man. He could hardly wait for that day to come.

The restless bleat of a sheep brought his mind back to the hillside. Quietly he slipped off the stump, and looked to where he heard the plaintive cry for help. A tiny lamb was caught in the thicket of low bushes. Aaron gently set the lamb free, guiding it until it had safely nestled next to its mother. As the boy returned to the stump of the olive tree, he noticed the moonlight glisten in the eyes of the shepherd Joshua who had raised his head to see if Aaron had properly cared for the tiny lamb. Joshua lowered his head back to the ground where he had been resting.

"He must have approved," thought Aaron to himself. Then he mused, "I'm certainly sorry Samuel is so sick tonight, but if he weren't, I might never have been asked to help with the sheep." Aaron was glad that he was counted among the needed shepherds while the new lambs were being born.

Aaron's right hand reached silently for the flute in his waist belt. With his left hand, he pulled the sheepskin tunic over his shoulders. The air was cooler at night. He tried to play a tune his father had taught him. The notes were there, but his fingers just wouldn't stretch far enough to cover the holes. He knew where to put them, but his small fingers just wouldn't reach. That didn't stop Aaron. The melodious notes he could play floated out into the silent night. As he played, Aaron's mind automatically returned to the lines of scripture that he had been memorizing during the week. The sight of the tiny town of Bethlehem brought to mind words from the book of Micah:

> "...O Bethlehem...who are one of the
> little clans of Judah, from you shall come
> forth for me one who is to rule in Israel,

whose origin is from of old, from ancient days" (Micah 5: 2 NRSV).

His mind shifted to words from Isaiah:

"Here is my servant, whom I uphold, my chosen, in whom my soul delights; I have put my spirit upon him; he will bring forth justice to the nations. He will not cry or lift up his voice, or make it heard in the streets; a bruised reed he will not break, and a dimly burning wick he will not quench; he will faithfully bring forth justice. He will not grow faint or be crushed until he has established justice in the earth; and the coastlands wait for his teaching." (Isaiah: 42: 1-4 NRSV)

Aaron stared at the star above him on the right. "Perhaps when the Messiah comes," he thought to himself, "he will be gentle as the scripture said. He won't shout, or quarrel, or tell children how small they are, or what they can't do." And as he was thinking, it was almost as if the hand of his father again touched his shoulder. As the feeling grew, the light above him seemed to grow. At first it was a shimmering; then it became a glow. Gradually the glow became a light, and then the light spread, almost like the light of day! Aaron heard the startled voices of the shepherds waking behind him as he raised the back of his hand to his face squinting at the light in the surrounding darkness.

What was he hearing? Angels, praising God, singing Gloria!

The music was clear and pure like no music he had ever heard. Aaron noticed the startled shepherds were now surrounding him. They crouched with fear, and even old Simeon was trembling. Aaron thought, "Maybe I should be afraid?"

Just then he heard a voice coming from an angel in the midst of the light.

> "...Do not be afraid; for see – I am bringing you good news of great joy for all the people: to you is born this day in the city of David a Savior, who is the Messiah, the Lord. This will be a sign for you: you will find a child wrapped in bands of cloth, and lying in a manger." (Luke 2: 10-12 NRSV)

Once again the angel's song filled the hillside.

> "Glory to God in the highest heaven, and on earth peace among those whom he favors!" (Luke 2:14 NRSV)

Aaron was the first to move after the voice was gone. The light faded.

"Simeon," he cried running to the old man, "did you hear? Did you see?"

Joshua, a younger man than Simeon, approached them, visibly shaken. His usual confident tones were hesitant.

"Simeon," he said, "let's go over to Bethlehem, and see if what we heard IS true!" Making a quick study of the stars in the sky, he added, "It's still the length of three temple services 'til dawn."

"Let's not wait until morning," Simeon answered. "If the message is true, it's too good to wait."

It was only a few moments until the sheep were safely secured and the excited shepherds were on their way down the hillside toward the still town of Bethlehem. From the midst of the moving silhouettes of the shepherds came the familiar notes of Aaron's flute.

"How do you suppose we'll find the child?" asked Joshua as the shepherds strode down the silent streets of Bethlehem.

"There's a lamp still burning at the inn," said Aaron as the shepherds rounded the corner. "And look, the innkeeper is out front putting out the lamps for the night."

"Run ahead and ask him," Simeon said quickly.

Although small, Aaron was a good runner and scarcely had the others taken a few steps when Aaron was already down the street at the Innkeeper's door. "Peace to you, Innkeeper," he began. "We're looking for a new baby born in Bethlehem this night. Have you heard of this child?"

"Peace to you young lad," said the Innkeeper, "and what keeps you up at this late hour?"

"I'm a shepherd this night, sir," said Aaron. "Samuel is sick. I was helping to tend the sheep on the hillside."

By now the other shepherds had arrived and greeted the innkeeper.

"A young couple came to our door this night,"

said the Innkeeper. "She was with child, and her time to deliver had come. I had no room, but they rest now behind the inn in the meager warmth of our stable. I was just going to take them this lamp, but if you care to take it to them, I'll finish closing the inn."

"We'll be happy to," said Simeon.

The Innkeeper handed the lamp to Aaron as he said, "Watch for the stones in the path."

Aaron felt the warmth of the light on his face, as he led the others carefully to the stable.

The small lamb Joshua carried in his arms bleated softly, announcing their presence as they approached.

"Peace to you," Aaron called softly inside as he reached the doorway.

"Peace to you," returned a warm voice as a man appeared at the door.

"We brought you a light from the Innkeeper," said Aaron, "with enough oil to last you well into the day."

"My name is Joseph," returned the man. "Would you care to come in?"

The lamp softly lit the room as Joseph led the shiny-faced shepherds to the feed trough where the baby lay. Simeon, Joshua, and Aaron looked at each other, nodding silently. It was as they had been told on the hillside. It was all true.

Mary was seated on a mound of straw. As each shepherd introduced himself, she smiled and gave a nod. As Aaron told his name, Mary noticed his waist belt and asked, "Do you play the flute?" He smiled and nodded.

"Yes, some."

"Would you play it for the new baby? We call him Jesus."

Aaron pulled the flute from his waist belt and began in soft tones. He played as well as his short fingers would allow. Mary smiled again. The baby stretched one tiny fist and then the other.

Joseph moved to the shadow and returned with a flute in his hand which he held out to Aaron.

"I made this here tonight in the stable while Mary was resting. I would like for you to have it, Aaron. It will be some time before Jesus is big like you to play it. And I'll have many other days to make him things in my carpenter's shop."

As soon as Aaron put the new flute to his mouth, sounds emerged which no one had ever dreamed possible. Simeon and Joshua looked at each other in utter amazement.

"He plays well," said Simeon.

"He is more than a good shepherd," said Joshua beaming.

"It is the right size for his fingers," said Joseph. "The Lord has given him a natural gift of music. All of us can help others by using the gifts the Lord our God has given us."

Aaron's face beamed as bright as the light from the oil lamp. He paused to take his own larger flute and let the tiny hand of the baby Jesus hold the end of it. "I'll leave this one for him," he whispered to Mary.

Dawn was now on the horizon heralding a new day. As the shepherds bid goodbye to their new friends and headed down the stone pathways of Bethlehem, people everywhere paused to take note of the beautiful music coming from the flute of the smallest shepherd.

Joshua and Simeon strode by Aaron's side with pride. They were glad that Aaron was from their hillside, and they knew that he would be a good shepherd.

*December 24, 1974*
*© Dr. Jerry Dickey*

"Aaron with the Innkeeper's Lamp"

# THE CHRISTMAS WREATH

## Story Three

hat can I make this year for Christmas?" thought Keisha Kelly to herself. She was surrounded by the smells of fresh baked cookies her mother was taking out of the oven in the next room. Part of the legacy passed to her from other generations was the tradition of setting aside money far in advance of Christmas, so that special gifts could be made – including the source of these delicious aromas. Keisha didn't know of anyone who made such unusual cookies and cakes as her mother. Cookie angels decorated with silver halos stood up on the plate on clouds of spun sugar. Christmas tree cakes were covered with green icing and sprinkled with powdery sugar-snow with tiny decorations in different colors on every branch. Homemade ice cream was in the shape of stars with king's crowns made of different colored sugars right in the center.

Keisha's eyes moved to the table and the manger scene her dad had made. He had taken the wooden vegetable boxes at the store and made each figure by hand. Her mother and grandmother had carefully made the clothes from scraps of cloth. Her eyes moved to the bell hanging from the floor lamp. Keisha had made it just one year ago today on her birthday. She remembered how hard she had worked to get the coat hangers in the right shape, and how she covered it with the bright red cloth her mother found from an old apron. It was well crafted for a little girl, she thought to herself, but today Keisha was eight, and she was certain she could do a grown-up job this year.

The screech of car brakes just outside the front window on Vine Street broke Keisha's thought. As the beautiful sounds of her favorite Christmas carol streamed from the radio, "Silent night, Holy night...," she jumped up and ran to the window, fearful of what she might see. She was thankful when there was nothing there. Although it was the middle of the day, it was cloudy and very cold. Down Vine Street she could already see some of the city lights twinkling against the dark sky.

"Keisha, I can sit down now and help you if you need me." It was the voice of Keisha's mother who entered the room with a smile.

"Mother, I'm not sure what to do this year," Keisha said as she flopped in a chair. "The only thing I do know is that I want to make a present to give away this year."

"You do?" responded her mother, "to whom?"

"I'm not sure, but to a lot of people, I think."

"Come sit on the couch with me," suggested Mrs. Kelly, "and let's look through this old Christmas book of Grandma's. Maybe you'll get an idea."

Keisha snuggled in close to her mother, and they began to turn the worn pages. "How come the Christmas trees all have white candles on them?" Keisha asked.

"That was before there were different colors of electric lights," her mother said softly, "but they were beautiful trees nonetheless – simply beautiful."

Keisha had to turn only one more page, and she had her project in place. It was a picture of an old store window where a big green Christmas wreath hung.

"Mother!" Keisha said excitedly. "Can I use some of the evergreen left over from the front porch?"

"Yes, we do have some," said her mother.

"Oh, good!" said Keisha, and she was off like a flash.

"What else will you need?" her mother said loud enough to keep up with Keisha's excitement.

"Something to make the wreath around, and something to make four candles out of," Keisha called from the back porch.

Mrs. Kelly got newspaper and wire and her basket of cloth pieces. They sat down on the living room floor. Keisha's mother knew she didn't need to help, but from experience, she also knew how helpful it was to have someone around for encouragement.

"Mother, I'm going to make a wreath with four candles just like the one at church." Keisha said as she began to make a circle out of rolled newspaper.

"You mean like the Advent wreath on the altar?"

"Yes," said Keisha, "What color are the candles, Mother?"

"There are three purple, one pink, and one white one in the middle." Mrs. Kelly responded. The colored ones mean we're preparing for Jesus, and the white one is for Jesus' birthday."

"Mother, do you have any white cloth in the basket?"

Mrs. Kelly searched through the scraps. "Do you want purple and pink too?"

"No, just white please."

Mrs. Kelly found a large piece of white felt. "How's this?" she asked.

"Oh, Mother, that's just right! Do you know what I'm making?" she said after a few minutes.

"What?" encouraged her mother.

"A wreath with four white candles like they used to use on Christmas trees, and I'm going to take it to Nathaniel Wilson's delicatessen 'cause he doesn't have anything for Christmas in the window!" After a short silence Keisha continued, "Mother, do you know what the four candles mean?"

"What do they mean?"

"They're my favorite Christmas carol," said Keisha. One stands for 'silent'. One stands for 'night.' One stands for 'Holy.'

"Do you have two candles for 'Night'?" her mother broke in questioningly.

"Oh, no," said Keisha, "the fourth one is 'light'... silent...night...holy...light."

Mrs. Kelly gave a pat to Keisha's black curls and walked toward the kitchen feeling a deep warmth that didn't come from the warm oven. She hummed the carol over and over again, but there were three words she just had to sing – "love's pure light."

With the project completed, Keisha put on her wool coat. It was cold outside. Keisha turned from the sidewalk to wave to her mother on the porch.

"Hurry back!" her mother called.

"Okay," she said, but she took a moment to drink in

the beautiful sight of the candles with flickering yellow bulbs in their two front windows, and the red bells aglow in the upstairs bedroom windows.

The Christmas wreath was nearly as big as Keisha. She was glad it was down hill to Mr. Wilson's delicatessen. She paused only a moment in front of the sign, "Westendorf's," lit in green, to look at the cone shaped paper tree that was turning round and round in the window. Mr. Wilson's shop was next door. He was a friend of Keisha's father, and was always glad to see her. He was visibly moved by the gift, and thanked Keisha, insisting she take a candy cane.

"I'm glad you like it, Mr. Wilson." said Keisha.

"Only trouble is, Keisha," Nathaniel Wilson said, "with your mother's suggestion, I doubt if I can keep it very long! And I'll be sure to tell people," he continued, "Silent Night, Holy Light!"

Keisha left the deli, carefully crossed the intersection by Al's Bargain Center, and wound her way up the street. It was getting dark as Keisha passed the red and green beer signs in the Curve Café. Then she passed the tall apartment building with red candles in red wreaths lit in each window of the second floor. She couldn't decide if she liked the red candle-wreaths better, or the red bells in her own house. It was almost a tie, she thought.

As she came upon the row houses made of red brick with black wooden porches where she lived, Keisha saw the silhouette of her father through the living room window. With excitement she happily raced up the stone steps and was near the top of the second flight of wooden steps to the porch when it happened. Whether it was ice, or bad footing, or the cover of night, or a combination of it all, no one knows, but there was a thud and Keisha was on the ground. Mr. and Mrs. Kelly were soon there, and Keisha hardly knew what happened. All she felt was the pain in her leg. They covered her with a blanket, and placed a pillow under her head. One tear glistened on the end of her nose.

It seemed like a long time to Keisha, but her dad said the ambulance was there in five short minutes. She could see the lights dancing on the snow like a merry-go-round, and as she was lifted on a board and then to a stretcher, she heard the siren begin. Usually cars zipped by on Vine Street like speeding rows of lighting bugs on a summer evening, but tonight each car paused as it passed, almost as if they wanted to stop and talk. As Keisha questioned the words, "Silent Night," in her mind, the loud siren continued. Then she thought of the baby Jesus in Bethlehem, and all the people, and noise, and no room. In the emergency room, everything became so bright, she could only think of how little light they must have had in the stable.

Mr. Kelly held Keisha's hand. "They're going to take a picture of your leg," he said.

Things seemed to move slowly in her mind, but a lot happened in two hours. It was a break in Keisha's lower left leg. The break was even, and though painful to a girl of eight, it was not bad in the eyes of the doctors. Soon her left leg was covered from foot to hip with a long white plaster cast. Moved from the emergency room to the hallway, Keisha began to put her good foot on the floor to test the new crutches when Mrs. Kelly heard Keisha yell, "Mother!"

Mrs. Kelly ran to her side and saw her sitting with her arm outstretched – finger pointing toward the wall. Keisha's eyes were as big as saucers, and her mouth was wide open. There on the wall was a large green wreath with four white felt candles!

Before either of them had a chance to say anything, the receptionist had taken the wreath off the wall, and was handing it to Keisha.

"I was told to give it to the first person who liked it," said the lady with a smile. She continued, "I'm supposed to tell you that the four candles stand for "Silent, Night, Holy..." And before she could say the fourth word, Mrs. Kelly and Keisha cried out at the same time, "Light!"

"How on earth did you know?" the lady asked surprised.

The receptionist's husband had stopped in Nathaniel Wilson's deli, and when Mr. Jones told Mr. Wilson how nice it was, it was given to him. It was in the back seat of the car when Mr. Jones picked up his wife to drive her to work at the hospital. When she commented on how beautiful it was, he told her that it was now hers. Mrs. Jones hung it in the emergency entrance way that Christmas Eve.

When the ambulance driver took Keisha home that night, he said how much he liked it, and it became his. He hung it in the back of the ambulance for someone else to have very soon. That had been Keisha's mother's suggestion:

"If someone said they liked it, it was to be given to that person to take, along with it's message. That way, many different persons could enjoy one present, for that's the way it was with God's present of Jesus."

As Keisha was carefully helped up the familiar wooden steps to their porch, she stopped and looked at her mother and father.

"You know why the Christmas wreath has to be a circle?" she said with a smile, "Because it never ends!"

And in the warmth of their living room, as Mr. Kelly turned on the radio they all smiled at each other as they heard..."Silent Night, Holy Light!"

*December 24, 1976*
*© Dr. Jerry Dickey*

"Keisha's Christmas Wreath"

# A GIFT OF HOPE

## Story Four

Mary Sue turned to her husband, Jack Edward, and sighed. "Tell me there is hope."

As in every person's life, there were moments when daily life seemed difficult and the future seemed bleak. He paused in silent support, put his arm around her shoulder, and said, "You sit by the girls' bed until you get tired, and then wake me."

She gave a pat to his right hand which was a unique gift from God, because at the last knuckle he had two thumbs. Jack Edward climbed into bed with all his clothes on and two pairs of socks, like a bear preparing for hibernation.

Mary Sue walked through the doorless frame to the next small room where three tousle-headed girls lay sideways across the bed. She gathered a few summer dresses from a cardboard box in the corner and tucked them carefully around each little arm and foot of her children. Then Mary Sue sat in the roughly hewn rocker, which her husband had carefully crafted by hand as a gift for last year's Christmas.

She laughed inwardly as she pulled an old chenille bedspread around herself. Her parents had taught her to laugh whenever things got difficult. It was a wonderful legacy for them to leave her. She began to rock. The motion helped to keep her feet warm. The tiny tap of her toes on the floor reminded her of the rhythm of the rotating sound of the rope on a tree limb when her little brother used to push her in the swing on warm summer days. He had died at age twelve, and for ten years Mary Sue placed a pine tree branch with a red ribbon on top of his grave. He had died two weeks before Christmas, when she was only fifteen, but she could remember his laughter pealing across the hillsides and the twinkle of his blue eyes under a haystack of golden hair. He was a brother, but unlike siblings in many families, he had also been her best friend.

Mary Sue looked over her shoulder to see the stars blinking in the moonlit sky through the small window. It had four panes. Last year it only had three and a piece of cardboard. That made it difficult in the winter when the cold winds blew around the mountain. Her mind relived the happy time last summer when a work group had swarmed around their house for a whole week like a busy hive of hornets. They had replaced the cardboard with a real piece of glass, covered the outside house boards with tarpaper, and built the nicest set of steps with the most beautiful hand railing she could ever imagine. Before that, the only way into their home was up a giant step to a box, and then up another giant step to the doorway.

Her vision of technicolor summer colors faded as she focused on the ice crystals formed in the corners of the windows. A moonbeam carved a light pattern in the top right corner just like the sunlight in summer on certain leaves in the shaded forest. "Hope," she thought to herself as she imagined the angel voices of Bethlehem settling in on the barren land around her own home. The coal company had left reddish tan plateaus where some of the hills had once stood. Trees and grasses would grow back, but that would take many years.

She thought of Joseph and Mary with only a donkey, plodding across a strip of desert land. She imagined them arriving at the doorstep of her own house, and the warm invitation she would offer them to step in away from the wind. "We don't have much," she would say, "but I can find some extra things in the box to keep you warm. Come in out of the weather. Do come in."

Mary Sue had moved to the side of the bed tucking the quilt around the girls when she returned from her visions that Christmas Eve. Checking the covers throughout the night was a nightly ritual for parents of small children in that vicinity. More than one child had frozen to death in the middle of the night by rolling out of the covers. When she had finished, she turned to go to the other room to waken Jack Edward for his turn to watch the girls. "I need to make sure he gives me the last morning shift," she thought to herself, "so he can go to Granny's early and bring the gifts back for the girls' Christmas."

Jack Edward was out the door at the crack of dawn – puffs of icy smoke spurting like a steam engine with every breath he took. "Kentucky is beautiful when the silent snow covers the earth," he thought to himself. He turned before he started down the dry creek bed – the only road up the holler to their house – to look at the silver tin foil star over the door, which Mary Sue and the girls had made. The winds turned it this way and that, forcing it to shimmer in the morning light.

As he began the descent from the middle of the mountain, he put his hands in his pockets and began to rub the two thumbs of his right hand against the first finger. It was like a pacifier to a child, or a warm, happy memory to an adult. His grandmother who raised him had so instilled in his mind how special and gifted Jack Edward was to have two thumbs on one hand, that all the taunts of school children when he was growing up, and the concealed stares of strange adults, never interrupted or changed that belief. He loved the quizzical stares with half-opened mouths, the questions people asked, and even those who made fun.

Granny Craig would say to him as he sat upon her lap as a child, "In all the world God has chosen you to be unique and gifted." She always reminded him, "You know, three thumbs are always better than two."

All of his life, gifted as he was, he looked for special gifts in others as well. Whenever he met people who considered themselves average or normal, he treated them as if they were very special people as well. However, he always wished that they too could have the wonderful thrill to believe they were unique, as he did.

As the creek bed neared the bottom of the mountain, Jack Edward saw Granny's cabin, but no smoke was coming from the chimney. His stomach clenched in a knot, and he swiftly shifted into a run, which took his thin body quickly to the house. He had hardly pushed the door open, when he saw her still body on the floor.

Her coat was on, and a water pail was on the floor beside her, so he knew that she had not been there long. He lifted her to the bed, felt a pulse, and ran to the Brenner's house down the road – the only one in the area with a phone. After she called the ambulance, Mrs. Brenner returned to Granny's with Jack Edward. She found a few bruises with some swelling, which she treated with a cold pack of chopped icicles in a thick washcloth. While they were waiting, she told Jack Edward that she would send her young neighbor, Paul Eric, up the holler to tell Mary Sue about Granny so that she would not be worried.

It was 11 o'clock Christmas morning before the ambulance arrived. Jack Edward climbed into the back with Granny and the nurse for the trip to the clinic. Granny drifted in and out of consciousness.

"The angels are finished and wrapped in a red cloth in a basket on the table," she said to Jack Edward. "I also have a letter I've been keeping for you in the front of my Bible," she continued feebly. Jack held Granny's hand, and counted telephone poles all the way to the clinic.

Granny Craig was a hardy soul, strong as the mountains. Her gentle eyes were in contrast to her unstoppable courage, her independent living, and her unending wisdom. She had to have been born of the spirit, because it was too deep to come from common human beings. It was she who slept with a shotgun under her bed in case rattlers crawled under the slit beneath the kitchen door seeking warmth in the winter night. It was she who took a bucket of water up a ladder at the back of the house before each meal to douse the roof so sparks from the stove would not set the house on fire. It was she who taught family and friends how to pray to the Lord. And every night she got on her knees.

Darkness was arriving by the time Jack Edward returned to Granny's house at the foot of the holler. Though she had not returned with him, the doctor seemed confident that a day's rest and observation would allow her to return home. The clinic staff had seen to it that Jack Edward had a large paper sack stuffed with popcorn balls, sugar cookies, and ribbon candy to take with him to his family.

He picked up the basket with the angels wrapped in the red cloth napkin. He lit a candle, opened the Bible, and pulled out the letter, which he began to read:

> Dear Jack Edward Craig,
>
> I am 84 and someday soon will join your grandpa. Some say we have had a difficult, hard life. I say if you know the Lord is there, then all you have to do is love yourself and laugh a lot, and life will always bring a smile to your lips and peace to your heart. When that time comes for me everything here is yours, but the memories are yours and mine together.
>
> Love, Granny

Jack Edward took the candle to the kitchen, dripped some wax into a giant pickle jar, and set the candle in it securely. Then he placed it on the front porch. A lighted candle for each member of the family was a Christmas tradition.

"This is your Christmas light, Granny," he said quietly but with strength. "I'm glad you're still here."

With a bundle of goodies under one arm and the basket of angels in the other, he quickly made his way up the familiar creek bed. Wash Creek glistened wherever the moon patches hit the snow, and at points, it sparkled like diamonds.

Five candles were gleaming in the window of his home off in the distance. He took the long way home, which was but five minutes out of his way. Up the pine-covered slope, the very top of the mountain was cleared of trees. It was like a sanctuary next to the twinkling, starry universe, his favorite place on the mountain. A Christmas carol echoed in his mind. As a boy, he had never heard the word 'Hark' before, and so he always thought the hymn said, "HOPE! The herald angels sing!"

"Thank you, God," he said, "for all the ways you give me Hope. Thank you for special gifts that you have given to me all through my life. And please continue to give me gifts I may share that will last beyond my own time."

Within moments, he was at his front door as the five candles twinkled in the window below the starlight. To his surprise, at the bottom of the sack given to him by the personnel at the clinic, there was a small canned ham, and some apples and nuts as well.

He shared the story of his day. And knowing that it was his favorite place, when Mary Sue asked that he tell them again about his stop at the sanctuary high on the mountain, he said with a smile she understood, "I stopped to tell the mountain that Jesus IS born."

The five angels were pulled from the basket one by one with apple doll faces and cornhusk dresses. The last one had a shirt and pants and one of the hands had two thumbs. As the candlelight dimmed, and cool air turned to cold, Jack Edward kissed the foreheads of his three little girls, and with a gentle hug and a tear in his eye, he said to Mary Sue, "Go to bed and rest. I'll wake you when it's time."

*December 22, 1989*
*© Dr. Jerry Dickey*

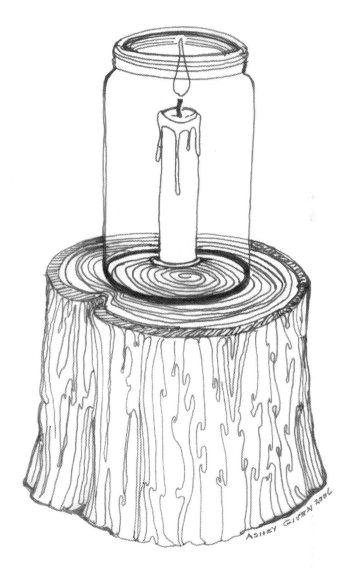

"Granny Craig's Candle in a Jar"

# THE UNEVEN GROUND

## Story Five

The uneven ground at the back of the homestead always held a great fascination for the twelve-year-old boy. Paul stood at the top of the long wooden steps leading from the back porch to the short cement walk that led to the garage. From the bottom of the wooden steps, six cement steps led back down under the porch toward a door on the left to the basement of the house. As he leaned on the hand railing, his vision swept out over the acre of land behind the old three story white wooden frame house. His eyes focused first on the bare limbs of the crab apple tree, then the currant bushes off to the right from which his mother made jelly each summer. He surveyed the roughly jagged soil at the very back of the family property to the left. The uneven soil stood out from the even, flat land around it like a dramatic melody sustained by a chorus that surrounds and supports it.

It was the end of November, but it felt like a warm Indian summer day in October. The breeze had just a hint of cool in the warm sun. His dark hair swiveled in twists as the breeze played with it that Sunday afternoon. He heard the faint sounds of the metal toy xylophone which his little sister Patsy played. She was tapping out single notes with a little hammer.

Though eight years apart in age, Patsy was the joy

of Paul's heart, and he always treated her specially. Shivers went up his spine as he focused back on the bottom cement step twelve feet below the open railing from the top of the wooden steps where he stood. It was just two and a half weeks ago that he had arrived home from school and found the note that his parents were at the hospital. Later he had learned that his redheaded little sister had fallen under the railing and cracked her forehead on a stone step below.

His eyes welled up with tears just imagining her fall, and the terrifying thought that she could have died. It was the first time he had been able to face the image of his little sister's pain since it happened. Before that, he just tried to avoid the image. He wished he could have taken her place; that's how much she meant to him. The metal sound of single notes on the xylophone which was his 1949 Christmas present to her just a year ago reminded him that she was alive and now on the mend. The stitches had been removed from her left forehead, but as her big brother, he made certain that everyone treated her with kid gloves.

It was the first Sunday in Advent, and though a twelve year old doesn't have a lot of motivation to consider thoughts from sermons, songs of praise, or Sunday School lessons, Paul had heard the word 'preparation' so much at church that morning that it had remained with him. His Sunday School teachers had used it, and the preacher, who was his father's close friend, had titled his sermon: "Prepare A Little Room." Paul's Sunday School teachers, Mr. and Mrs. Moffat, had talked about the prophet Isaiah and how he had worked so hard for his own people that it had helped others through the centuries as well.

Paul knew personally how hard life was for a twelve year old. Though he had many friends, now and then someone would make fun of him. Sometimes he couldn't run as fast as they could, or sing on pitch, or pass the football as consistently as some of his teammates. Inside, he simply didn't understand why people had to give others a hard time, or make fun of others, since he did not do that himself.

Paul walked to the bottom of the steps and stood on the path between the steps and the garage. In the distance, he heard church bells as his eyes returned to the uneven ground. That's the way *he* felt today – a little uneven.

The words which opened the church service, and which were used a number of other times throughout the morning, filled his mind with its haunting repetition–

"PREPARE YE THE WAY OF THE LORD…
PREPARE YE THE WAY OF THE LORD…"

Paul knew that's what Advent was – preparation – but every year the lights and presents and bells and trumpets prepared everybody for something wonderful. Then wars and hatred and teasing words started all over again, and it seemed as if everyone was always preparing for something that never arrived. He couldn't believe that God always wanted us to be on the road and never at the party.

He heard the clop, clop of Patsy's shoes coming down the back wooden stairway to the kitchen. He turned and walked back up the top steps to the enclosed porch and then through the open kitchen door.

Patsy walked across the kitchen. Her blue and white skirt with crinolines flopped back and forth like waving grain in a wheat field on a windy day. She clambered up onto a wooden kitchen chair. Her long-sleeve white blouse had tiny embroidered blue and green flowers on the collar. Patsy looked up at Paul with her forlorn eyes, and Paul *knew* he was going to have to help with something. "What's the matter?" he asked.

She set the metal music box on the table. "My music box lady is broken," she said. Then with her right hand, she spread what looked to Paul like chunks of white dust and some other bits and pieces on the kitchen table.

"Oh, Patsy," he said, "I'm sorry."

"The angel broke all to pieces," she said, so softly he almost had to read her lips.

Paul wished he had the right words as his father always said the preacher had in church; but since he didn't, he instinctively wound up the music key in the metal base. It played, 'Joy to the World.'

With her still forlorn eyes she said to Paul, "Will you bury the angel with Missy, my cat?"

Their parents wouldn't be back for an hour, and since Paul was the man of the house and the only present decision maker, he found an empty cigar box. Taking a shovel and the cigar box full of angel dust in his left hand, and Patsy's hand in his right, they set off across the smooth yard to the uneven ground.

He couldn't remember where Missy was buried, but he pretended to, and then moved over a couple of steps. He gave Patsy the cigar box and started to dig. Two shovels of dirt had been removed when Paul heard a clunk on the third. He tried to move what he thought was a rock, but after working at it, found an iron metal box with a little copper trim that was now green. He decided to keep attending to his sister's present needs, and set the box to the side even though he was curious about what he found. Paul carefully placed the cigar box in the freshly dug space and gently covered it with dirt. He leaned over to give his sister a little hug. Patsy stood on her tiptoes and gave her brother a kiss on the cheek. A swell of wind tossed his hair and pressed against his shoulders like a pat on the back. He knew he had helped his little sister prepare for another day.

Patsy's shoulder length pony tail swung back and forth like the windshield wiper on the car in the rain, as she and her big brother walked hand in hand back to the big white frame house. The strawberry blonde highlights of her hair glistened in the sun. When they had put the shovel in the garage, they climbed the high stairway back to the kitchen. Paul put the iron box on the table and took two satiny white pieces of his mother's homemade taffy from the pink glass cookie jar. It was ample reward to taste the Karo-based sweetness sliding down his throat. Patsy chewed hers in silent pleasure, her big brown eyes calm, happy, and reflective like a doe in a grassy field in the springtime.

Paul placed their tiny wax taffy papers in the wastebasket under the sink, and turned to the box. He had already wiped it off, and the hook came open easily as he handled it with wonderment.

"What is it?" questioned Patsy, now as intensely involved as her older brother.

"There's some crinkly papers all wrapped up in a cloth!" came his reply.

He felt both ease and excitement – the same feeling he had when he turned from the stone covered alley onto the soft, level green grass of his backyard on the way home from school in the springtime. There was a quiet anticipation on Patsy's face, as her brother opened the two pages. The first was a letter of sorts, and the second, a page of scripture. Paul began to read aloud:

> From James W. Ellsworth
> December 11, 1831
> I am eighty-seven years old, and have traveled across many lands, but none is more beautiful than the place where you are seeing your final sunsets. I came to America with my parents, Wilson D. and Constance Davis Ellsworth. All my family is gone, and their legacy now rests with me. Arriving when I was 18 years of age, my family lived first in Maryland, then in Pennsylvania, and then Ohio. With the help of Indian friends of Tecumseh,

I built a mill by the river, and ran the gristmill on land, which is known as the highest point between the Appalachians and the Rockies. In these latter years since the mill was destroyed, I have spent time leveling this beautiful land, which was in no place level, into a smooth plain. In the corner, however, I have left part of the land as it was. I call it the uneven ground. It is there as a symbol of the year the Circuit Rider stayed at our home during a blizzard. I had buried a daughter, a son, and my wife. My two remaining sons and I battled sickness, hardship, and difficulties of every kind. Some days it seemed as if all of life was against us. The parson told me it would change if I were to spend as much time preparing my heart as I did this land. He was right. That year when he left my home on December the 8th, the child of Christmas remained. I pray that this land will be a blessing to all who live upon it, and that the uneven ground will be a symbol of hope to you for what God can do with our hearts.

On the second page were words from the 40th chapter of Isaiah:

"...in the wilderness, Prepare ye the way of the Lord,...Every valley shall be exalted, and every mountain and hill shall be

made low:...and the rough places plain:"
(Isaiah 40: 3,4 KJV)

Paul reached up to the shelf next to his mother's cookbooks where they kept their family Bible. He opened the book to Isaiah where he read from the newer version the words that would become meaningful to their family for years to come: "...the uneven ground shall become level, and the rough places a plain" (Isaiah 40:4 RSV).

When Paul and Patsy's parents returned, Paul was praised for how well he had handled everything that day. His parents were enthralled with the box and the letters. The letters were framed and hung in the kitchen near the window overlooking the uneven ground.

Years later, in 1981, 150 years after the letters in the box had been written, both Paul and Patsy had prints of those letters made into Christmas cards which were sent to family, friends, and co-workers across the country and around the world.

*December 9, 1990*
*© Dr. Jerry Dickey*

"The James W. Ellsworth Cabin"

# THE CHRISTMAS CHURCH

*Story Six*

Al - le - lu - ia. Alle - lu - u - ia. Alle - lu - u - ia." The radio sang out the joyful chorus before old Minerva Clump could do her three-step hobble with a cane across the floor to bring the angelic airwaves to a halt with a click.

"F-f-f-f-t," she said like a cat caught in a corner. Just at that moment the well-used round metal doorbell fastened within the big wooden front door just below the window was given a turn.

"Bl-l-l-l-l-t," it resonated half-ringing and half-sputtering.

She turned and scooted toward the door, her robe, housecoat and shawl giving her a foreboding appearance. The postal carrier stood strong, lips together, determined. It was the only way she could get through the next few moments. It was as though the post office had given everyone special training for the Clump house.

"Mrs. Markee," Minerva began before the woman had a chance to state her business, "there was snow on my mail yesterday so once again you left the mailbox lid up. I hate wet letters!"

Peggy wasn't a "Mrs." She NEVER left Minerva's mailbox lid up in either sunshine or snow. And the only thing she left in Minerva's mailbox yesterday was a flyer from a furniture outlet. Why, even junk mail authors tried to avoid this address!

"I'm sorry," Peggy Markee said quickly, to allow her to get to her task. "You have a postage due letter," she said factually.

If Peggy had left it in the mailbox with an envelope with postage due amount on it, Minerva would never have put out the change, and would have surely denied the whole issue. Peggy knew a letter would be her only excitement in weeks, so she had played it just right.

"A minute," Minerva huffed.

Minerva pushed the door nearly shut because she wasn't about to let anyone know where she kept her coin box. Peggy stood on the stoop with the wind whistling around her ears while Minerva took her time. Finally the door opened. Minerva handed her the change, and grabbed the letter.

"Merry Christmas," Peggy offered in hope.

The door slammed putting an exclamation point to her silence.

Minerva moved slowly toward the stuffed chair with lace doilies on the arms. The town clock was striking four. She sat, turned up the lamp a notch in the somber room, and reached for the letter opener with the Viking ship on the handle. It had been a Christmas present to her husband years before. She pulled out the letter along with a large newspaper article, a church bulletin, and a funeral home folder. Her heart became like ice. Her baby sister had died at eighty-two in Phoenix. She stood shaking, turned to the bureau, and pulled open one drawer after the other. At the back of the bottom drawer, she pulled out the dusty family Bible. She sat slowly, opened the book, and ran her finger over the carefully scripted words – Mildred Noelle Clause – and in parentheses, which was added later (Wright) – Born December 15, 1909. On a bookmark in her sister's handwriting was written: John 1:11-13. Slowly, she turned the long forgotten pages until she came to the words:

> "He came unto his own, and his own received him not. But as many as received him, to them gave he power to become the sons of God, *even* to them that believe on his name: Which were born, not of blood, nor of the will of the flesh, nor of the will of man, but of God." (KJV)

Rev. John Robert Klein had been a youth pastor at Central United Methodist Church in Harbortown for three years now. Kristin, Bob's wife, was a social/health worker for their state senator, and she had just returned home from a demanding day. The hall clock sounded half past four as Kristin dusted the snow off her coat.

"I made good time today," she said as Bob came bounding down the stairs.

"I'm always glad when you're safe at home," he said as he gave her a gentle bear hug and a kiss on the nose. "I worry about you on snowy roads."

"Worry won't melt snow," she said with a wry smile. Her brown eyes twinkled as she shook her dark brown hair like a wet pup. "I am lucky to have someone who really cares," she added.

Bob sat on the second to last stair step, and rested his head on his hands and his elbows on his knees. He looked at her admiringly.

"I will build you up and encourage you," were his words of response.

They were words from their wedding vows, which they had written together, and which both of them had memorized for all time.

The sound of quick footsteps and a nervous knock interrupted them. Stewart Cross and his daughter, Jennifer, were standing in their entranceway.

"Bob, Kristin," Stewart began in a rush, "Judy's gone, and I have a hospital patient who needs me. Can Jennifer be with you for an hour?"

"Sure," Bob said, "If we have to go somewhere we'll take her along."

Stewart was off before he arrived.

"Well, Jennifer probably wouldn't enjoy running errands with me," Kristin said.

"I have one shut-in call to finish before dark," Bob reflected, "old Minerva Clump. I haven't met the person capable of handling that challenge! Well, Jennifer," he added taking her hand, "you'll get a star in your crown for *this* visit."

And before the snowflakes could melt on Jennifer's nose, Rev. Bob had his coat on, and he and Jennifer were off.

"It may not be so bad after all," Kristin called after them, "remember ... 'And a little child shall lead them.' "

As Bob climbed into the driver's seat of the goldenrod

Gremlin, he whispered to himself almost in prayer, "Only God can lead old Mrs. Clump!"

The clock was striking five as Minerva heard the half-ringing, half-sputtering of her doorbell. The first words Bob heard were, "It's only three days until Christmas. I'd given up on anyone from the church showing up!"

Bob thought to himself: "That's how a bleating lamb must sound when it's lost in the wilderness." But he was used to such obstinate words from Minerva, and he nestled Jennifer next to him on the settee in an attempt to protect her from the bitter environment.

No one remembers how it happened, but somewhere between Rev. Bob's concerned questions and Minerva's caustic, blunt remarks, she mentioned her sister had died. Something in the child responded to the old women. Perhaps it was because Jennifer's favorite cat had recently been run over and she knew how grief felt, or maybe the pathos in Minerva's voice had touched her spirit. The little girl immediately slid off the settee, walked across the room, climbed up and snuggled in beside the woman. She reached her little arm up across Minerva's shoulder, and gently began patting her hair.

There are some things you couldn't pay to achieve in life. Minerva shed one large Christmas tear, but withheld her life's floodgates, which had for years been saving up to break.

When Rev. Bob and Jennifer got in the car, Jennifer leaned over and asked why the lady had a big tear in her eye. And Bob simply said, "I think you made her very happy, Jennifer. It was a happy tear."

Minerva had held her tears back until they left, but now she sat helplessly crying herself into the Kingdom.

Jennifer went home. Kristin had finished her errands. At dinner, Bob shared with Kristin the "touching big tear experience" at Minerva's.

The phone rang. Kristin could always tell when there was a crisis by the way Bob held the phone. "Okay," was all Bob said. He hadn't even put the phone down on the receiver. "Come on, Kristin. I think the old woman's dying," were his words.

Minerva had heard Rev. Bob's comments before the phone clicked.

"Good! Thanks for your help, God," she said. "He thinks I'm dying! Well, I have," she exclaimed to herself. "I died tonight, and I was born all over at the same moment! The only difference between me and old Lazarus is they won't have to help unwind all the old strips of burial cloth!"

A giggle came to her throat. If anyone had seen her, they would have thought her mad. She was hobbling in noticeable dance steps across the room without her cane. Her arms were swinging in rhythm with her mind.

From the antique clapboard, she found an old red cellophane wreath with an electric candle and quick as a flash had it hanging in one of the front windows. She gave the plug a push into the socket, and plunk, on came the light.

"That in itself is a miracle," she said to herself as she giggled in response to the light.

She brought a doll from the closet, a teddy bear from

the shelf, and a toy soldier long lost in a roll-top desk drawer. The room was re-born with magic.

Cups were out, "washed from centuries of neglect!" she again spoke to herself, and chuckled in response. "I've talked to myself for years," she said continuing to giggle, "only finally, I'm starting to make some sense!"

Who knows how she did it, except through the power of the God of Christmas, everything is possible. The round table was set with three large place mats, three cups and saucers, tiny salt saucers with a puff peppermint ball as a place marker, and a sugar bowl full of cinnamon sticks. A beautiful orange was on each plate as the main course.

Bob and Kristin slid through the two-inch snow on the walkway to Mrs. Clump's doorway. The Christmas wreath candle tipped them off to be wary.

"Minerva?" Bob called as he opened the door in both fear and wonder.

Once inside, Kristin and Bob felt the transformation as if they had entered into the dream world of the first Christmas, transferred by two centuries of culture and change. The stale room of two hours ago was aglow with sights and smells and sounds. And on a mirror in the center of the table was a doll, in a cloth, resting on straw that looked like it had been cut from a broomstick.

One hour later, Bob and Kristin were leaning toward Minerva, arms crossed on the table in front of them, listening intently to the power of love transforming the world in which we live. "From now on everyone can call me 'Minnie C.,' " she said. "That's what I was called as a child. I want to be a 'Minnie' Christ, and even when I can't get to church, I'm going to be the church!" She leaned forward and questioned hopefully, "What do you think of my plan?"

It was Thursday night, and on Sunday morning everyone from the town would come to the church for traditional Christmas Day services.

The plan unfolded like clockwork. That Thursday evening, Bob carried Minnie C. to their car, and the three of them drove to church where the other pastors met them. They took her from room to room in a wheelchair, describing who met there each Sunday, while Minnie C. took notes and drew pictures. She had twelve years of 'ohs' and 'ahs' to make up for.

Back at Minnie C's house, Bob made a phone call to one person from his prayer/study group.

"Jane, tell the group some flowers are needed right away. We'll meet at Minerva Clump's tomorrow at 6 PM for sandwiches and assignments."

The word "flowers" was their signal for a crisis, and no group worked harder at a crisis than this prayer/study group. Friday night, two days before Christmas, eleven of fourteen showed up at Minnie C's. In 36 hours, the preparations the group had made, led by Minnie, were complete.

Over every doorway on Christmas Sunday morning, people saw signs as they entered their church, which read, "THE CHRISTMAS CHURCH." And no matter what room they entered that day there was a tree, and each one was decorated with thoughtful little gifts for the ages of the persons meeting there. On the top of each tree was an electric candle, with a banner near the top reading, "YOU CANNOT REALLY GIVE UNTIL YOU RECEIVE. A JOY-FILLED CHRISTMAS FROM JESUS, AND JENNIFER, AND MINNIE C."

For all the remaining days she lived, Minnie C's house was a joy-filled blessing for all. And many noticed that as she listened to others, she always put her arm on their shoulders, and patted their hair.

*December 14, 1991*
*© Dr. Jerry Dickey*

"Minerva and Jennifer"

# THE FIRST CHRISTMAS JOURNEY

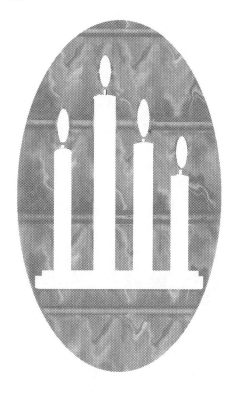

*Story Seven*

The donkey stood motionless on the dry land. Stale air engulfed it, and aching stillness clogged its ears like thick cotton. Nothing had been heard or seen for days. Foraging for food through sparse clumps of wild grass left little hope for life to change in this wilderness. Evening brought the quick cold of night's blackened cover. Starlight highlighted the donkey's lean rib cage and one bright ray caught the left eye of the animal as it drifted into sleep.

Morning brought an abrupt halt to numbness as the donkey felt a tug on the grayed stub of rope still attached to its worn harness.

"Come on," spoke a warm, gentle voice, "you are a gift of grace from the Lord. You shall make the journey possible."

The voice led, and the weary beast instinctively followed without much thought or question. The tall, strong man stroked the donkey's neck with his right hand as he passed the short rope-stubble to his left hand. The last time the donkey remembered being touched by anything other than tall rocks at the edge of the desert, was the joyful touch of children shortly after it had been born. Though its empty stomach ached, there was a tinge of caring warmth that even a beast of burden could feel.

The journey was not more than an hour to Nazareth.

Joseph stopped at the carpenter's shop and tied a new, long, thin rope to the donkey, which had plenty of lead. He then tethered the other end of the rope to a wooden hook on the wall of the shady side of the house, placed a large handful of straw and another of wheat on the ground, and then brought a small wooden trough which he set down and filled with water.

"Eat well, my friend," Joseph said, "you are to carry precious cargo to Bethlehem on tomorrow's journey!"

The donkey drank gratefully as Joseph went into the house.

When Joseph entered the cozy, small room, he wrapped Mary gently in his arms. She rested her head on his chest and sighed deeply.

"The donkey was right where the men of the caravan told me they saw it," he began. "Those sages on their camels have been a great blessing to us. The light of the Lord has made our pathway brighter. Yesterday, the journey was still a foreboding one. Today, it looks possible. You will not have to walk to Bethlehem."

Joseph felt a wet tear on his hand as Mary began to speak.

"Joseph, you know how persons of Nazareth, and the men of Israel, will look down upon you if I do not walk while you ride the donkey," she said. He held her shoulders with outstretched arms and smiled,

"There are many things we have already done differently," he said. "God's ways have been made known through prophets, priests, sages, and faithful persons common as the endless sands of the desert. God's ways are not our ways, and there are many things we will have to do differently in the future. Servants are often those who are not necessarily right, but faithful."

"I cannot do the Lord's work without you," Mary replied.

"Very few can do the Lord's work alone, Mary. The one who is called Messiah will call us from ourselves, and lead us to each other. It begins with us, and many unlike us, but the journey for all leads to God's kingdom. Think of the story of Ruth. She is part of the house of David in which I was born. Her faithfulness did more for the house of Israel than all of the judges and kings. If we focus on God, Mary, the eyes of the people who search for what is wrong, will be refocusing through us, on what God is revealing new. No, you WILL ride the donkey, Mary, and I will walk."

Enfolding her in his arms again, Joseph said in quiet afterthought, "If it will make you feel better, I'll ride the donkey to the edge of town."

Mary gave Joseph a squeeze, and sighed again, and then laughed.

It was called a beast of burden. It was an appropriate name, for no animal knew burden more than this donkey. Where children had once petted and played with the humble animal when very young, mistreatment and utter disregard for decent care had plagued its middle years of life. It had known hunger and beatings from humans who were disgruntled with their own lives. It had been tied tightly to a post facing a building, where the sweet tasting grass was beyond its reach, and the grandeur of the earth and sky created for all living things was removed from its vision. The donkey's stare had settled endlessly in the sand. It had lived for years in anonymity – overworked, underfed, maligned, and mostly ignored.

It was Sabbath and Joseph went alone to the synagogue. He left Mary at home to rest for what he knew would be a demanding journey for her. Quirinius' decree that they return to Bethlehem was neither timely nor thoughtful, for Mary's nearness to bearing the child would be a challenge, and Bethlehem's inadequacy to greet so many returning guests was certain to become a difficulty for all. At moments like these, Joseph eagerly met the Sabbath knowing the Lord God would speak again in comfort and direction to his faithful heart. Joseph entered the small synagogue in Nazareth and sat on one of the benches he himself had created at his carpenter's shop. Reflexes sent his hands along the smooth edges of the bench reminding him with assurance of the perfection and care with which his work was always completed.

The rabbi was a friend to Joseph, the Pharisee who, with humility and strength, would one day teach Mary's child of God's messianic gift to the world. The rabbi's name was Daniel, son of Eliphaz, and a distant cousin of Joseph. As Daniel went to the front of the synagogue and retrieved the scrolls, he turned to the gathered congregation, and his eyes smiled as he inwardly acknowledged Joseph's presence. The scroll today was opened to the words of Isaiah. Many nights Joseph and Daniel had sat and discussed these words outside the synagogue, or on smooth, hand-hewn stools made by Joseph and placed in the same spot where the donkey was now tethered so as to avoid the heated rays of the setting sun. Daniel's words reverberated in the small room:

> "Thus says the Lord: 'Keep justice, and do righteousness, for soon my salvation will come, and my deliverance be revealed. Blessed is the man who does this, and the son of man who holds it fast, who keeps the Sabbath, not profaning it, and keeps his hand from doing any evil.' Let not the foreigner who has joined himself to the Lord say, 'The Lord will surely separate me from his people;' and let not the eunuch say, 'Behold, I am a dry tree.' For thus says the Lord: 'To the eunuchs who keep my Sabbaths, who choose the things that please me and hold fast my covenant, I will give in my house and within my walls a monument and a name better than sons and daughters; I will give them an everlasting name which shall not be cut off. And the foreigners who join themselves to the Lord, to minister to him, to love the name of the Lord, and to be his servants, every one who keeps the Sabbath, and does not profane it, and holds fast my covenant – these I will bring to my holy mountain, and make them joyful in my house of prayer; their

burnt offerings and their sacrifices will be accepted on my altar; for my house shall be called a house of prayer for all peoples. Thus says the Lord God, who gathers the outcasts of Israel, I will gather yet others to him besides those already gathered.' "
(Isaiah 56:1-8 RSV)

On the first day of the week before dawn, Joseph untied the donkey, set the two sheepskin knapsacks of supplies with tethers across the donkey's shoulders, handed Mary the lead rope and walking stick, and said quietly to Mary, "Are you certain?"

She smiled and said, "The early hours are the best. I am strong."

Joseph placed himself on the donkey, and Mary led the donkey and her husband through the shadows of Nazareth. Joseph would have had her save even the littlest bit of strength for the journey, for as far as he could see, the only hint of light was from Elizabeth's home on the edge of town. She had gotten up in the middle of the night to bake her specialty – warm unleavened bread rolled in a sauce of figs, dates, and raisins. Neatly wrapped in clean, white cloths, Elizabeth carefully tucked her delicacy in the closest knapsack, kissed Mary on the forehead, and waved as the holy family's silhouettes faded into the wilderness shadows.

Mary was correct about the stares of strangers, once Mary mounted the donkey when they were beyond sight of Nazareth. But she was comforted by the strength of Joseph's earlier words, as well as with the response of one older woman winnowing in the fields near Bethlehem. She quickly offered a kind smile and a touching "Shalom" as she saw Mary's heavily pregnant figure passing by on the donkey behind Joseph.

But no woman of this day could relate to Mary's thoughts. Burdened with pain of movement, and the relentless struggle of being jostled about on the donkey's lean flesh, her mind had returned to Gabriel's bidding that she would bear a son, and the words ran over and over in her mind and voice: "My soul magnifies the Lord." The repetitious rhythm of these words fought the pain and disengaged her struggling mind.

The donkey plodded along, never faltering or slowing its pace. It is amazing how quickly kindness and good nourishment replenishes a battered will with strength. Mary was not heavy to the donkey. Life had become favorable in a few short days, and with each passing hour, the donkey knew both freedom and purpose. Joseph had a way of knowing – almost with spiritual telepathy – when to move Mary's legs from one side of the donkey to the other, and when to stroke the donkey's neck.

"The donkey is a blessing," she said to Joseph more than once.

"The Lord has shown us favor," Joseph echoed.

As they continued up the hauntingly familiar streets of Bethlehem, Joseph, Mary, and the donkey longed for time to slow down. They did not know, however, that because of their entry into Bethlehem, time WOULD stand still in coming centuries. The donkey continued steadfastly walking up the starlit streets, past the inn too crowded with people, right into the stable, which though seemingly meager in human terms, was a donkey's dream of comfort and rest and nourishment.

In the darkness of that night, lamplight alone reflected Mary's final birthing struggles, and then revealed a holy, helpless hint of God's love wrapped in swaddling that once held Elizabeth's tempting, healthful delicacies. Now nestled in straw, that white, brushed, soft wool protected this new life of all earth's future. Joined by the cattle's lowing, and the sheep's bleating, the donkey, formerly lost and alone in the world's wilderness, was the only godparent. The donkey had traveled from Nazareth to newborn child and had witnessed the wondrous gift. Words from scripture alone would honor the lowly beast of burden. They were words that would become God's gift to the struggling, pain-bearing, esteem-sacrificing humanity through the centuries to follow:

> "Thus says the Lord God, who gathers the
> outcasts of Israel, I will gather yet others
> to them besides those already gathered."

Even as Joseph spoke, a lamb softly bleated and camels gently plodded toward the Light of Bethlehem.

*December 18, 1992*
*© Dr. Jerry Dickey*

"Mary and Joseph's Christmas Journey"

# THE CHRISTMAS FRIEND

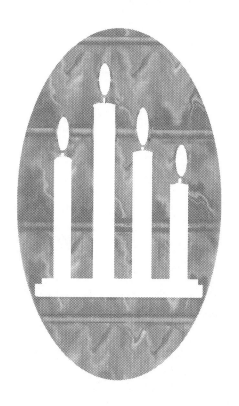

*Story Eight*

Hope was in John's mind this Christmas Eve. It wasn't that life for him was any easier. But somehow in the midst of the darkness, light held its faint hopeful ray through a twinkle of starlight, the streetlights, and even from the shining headlights that aimed triple laser-like beams onto the hood of his car. In the midst of isolated darkness and the unknown, all of these seemed to say that hope might continue to open up the future toward understanding, new birth, and perhaps, room at the inn.

The cold of the night brought back a reminder of the chill within him during moments in high school when he had contemplated taking his own life. There were a number of times when he thought life was too demanding. There were times when he had felt so left out and alone. There were times when in all the long list of admirers and friends, he had no one who could objectively listen to his story. He had sorely needed someone who understood and encouraged his perspective.

John was a natural in two areas: baseball and music. In high school, he had set records for home runs and runs batted in. He was known as a person who could set things right in a pinch, and also as one who could set aside his own glory and help make it happen for someone else. His senior year, attendance at their ball games had been twice that of other years, and although he attributed it to team effort and enthusiasm, most people acknowledged John as the singular catalyst.

In music, his strong bass voice won him State ensemble and solo recognition. His singing at school and church brought happy memories to adults who reminisced through him about their "good old days" when they could "understand the words." It also broadened the interest of his sports buddies. They paid more attention to his music because of the respect they had for him as a nearly unsurpassed athlete.

John had grown up with a deep faith. His Evangelical Covenant Church had been the center of warm faith feelings as a boy. He remembered at nine singing "SWEET HOUR OF PRAYER" as his first church solo. As he sang, he vividly remembered seeing the tears trickling down the cheeks of Mr. Westland, his Sunday School teacher. As an only child, his parents considered his voice one of God's many miracles, since neither of them could carry a tune. And whether it was sports or music, they were there for every game or musical performance in grade school, junior high, high school, and now, at the university.

This would be the seventh year in a row John would sing "O HOLY NIGHT" for the Christmas Eve candlelight service. His sophomore year in high school, he had been nervous, but after that first year, as the rich notes rolled along the brown wooden rafter beams, the awe-filled silence from the congregation was such that one felt as if the inside of the church might suddenly have been stilled with a foot of snow.

The last two years, John would rather not have sung "O HOLY NIGHT," but he knew what it meant for his parents and the community, so he pushed himself to sing, as a personal gift to them. Since John had gone to college in Chicago, he hadn't been attending any church regularly. Often, when he was in a church, it was in the middle of a week when he would find a cathedral door open, and he could go in and quietly sit by himself. His favorite time was when he happened into a church or a cathedral while the organist was in rehearsal. As the brass trumpet pipes bellowed or the fluted string sounds wafted among the rafters or stone ceilings, he would feel a comfort as if all the parts of his life fit together for a short time during those few moments of spiritual nourishment.

Life tends to keep most of us busy and occupied as we grow. But it doesn't always provide the necessary time for personal reflection that allows us to find the depth of ourselves that is both past-uplifting, present-revealing, and future-directing. As John drove down the freeway toward the outskirts of Indianapolis, the cold winds blew intermittent dots of snow against the windshield of his Jeep. He was about to deal once again with the double-edged sword of Christmas which brought together the warm faith of his upbringing, and the cold isolation of those unknowing people who thought they knew him so well.

Entering the large sanctuary, people were already filling the pews long before the hour of worship on this special night. John had hardly entered the door when handshakes, hugs, and smiling faces were warming him from the frosty night. High school friends who had not seen him since last summer's city league ball games, left their families for a few moments to greet him warmly. Bob Broderick came back to let John know that he and his wife were saving two places for John's parents down front where they usually sat on Sundays.

"Have you set the wedding date yet?" Bob continued.

The Brodericks lived next door to John's parents. He had been two years ahead of John in high school, and was also a good athlete, although not as strong, handsome, or charismatic as John. For as long as John had known him, that seemed to be Bob's opening line.

"Not yet," John smiled, "but the young lady I'm going with this year at school could well be the right one! She's as nice as your Nancy."

"That's great. I knew the Lord wouldn't let you down," Bob returned with a wave as he started back down the aisle. "We sure want to meet her. We'll be praying for you!"

John spent the next half hour in the small room off the choir room warming up. Having recently finished solo work with the University Glee Club for their Christmas concerts, his voice felt fine. He was also warmed by the greetings of friends. It relaxed him to know that there would be persons up front whom he knew well. It would allow him the feeling of singing this great song of faith to friends.

By now it was seven o'clock, and the 70-voice choir was beginning its rehearsal. John put on the blue robe that had his name hung on the hanger, and slipped in with the bass section. The choir director, Winton Hill, waved and smiled at John in an uninterrupted gesture while turning the page to continue rehearsing the MESSIAH with the choir.

The large sanctuary was filled as usual. The special lighting, the smell of pine, the flickering candles – all these brought back a memory of less complicated times of boyhood.

The entrance anthem of "GATHER YE PEOPLE, SING CHRISTMAS JOY" began the worship, and warmth overflowed. Prayers and portions of the MESSIAH, and a touching portrayal of a drama, "No Room at the Inn," by high school youth, preceded the Christmas offering which was to support a city homeless shelter and an overseas missionary to Russia. This was to be followed by the sermon, and then John would sing "O HOLY NIGHT" as the congregation lit individual candles.

John's mind was attentive during the sermon, but it had drifted a little when Dr. Willis zapped his heart back to reality with his electric-like probes of misinterpreted scripture.

"And we all agree," he continued, "that no homosexual can truly kneel at the Christ Child's feet unless his heart and his lifestyle is permanently changed."

No matter where it happened, whenever the word 'homosexual' came up in condemnation, John's body froze. He had heard it too many times. And since he was gay, it shot through his body like electricity. To hear it again on Christmas Eve was almost too much. John's heart raced like an automobile engine with the gas pedal stuck to the floor. All that he could think of was that he was glad that he wore a robe so his breathing wouldn't show. He was careful not to flinch, to change his gaze, or make a movement of any kind.

He hardly heard the rest of the sermon. But it settled for certain in his heart that this would be the last time he would sing in his home church. He knew at that moment that he could no longer sing to the people gathered there tonight, even his parents. His mind struggled to work, to think, to patiently seek to bring order out of chaos. He decided that tonight, he could only sing for all the men and women – past, present, and future – who so quietly had to be stripped of selfhood throughout life as gay people. He would sing for all these unknown soldiers of the faith, women and men who had been victimized and terrorized by such well-intended ignorance.

When the sermon ended, he stood. The lights dimmed. Restless movement subsided. The piano began quietly. John began gently:

"O HOLY NIGHT! THE STARS..." He thought of all the unknown disciples, church leaders, and servants of history who, like himself, had been born gay. "...ARE BRIGHTLY SHINING, IT IS THE NIGHT OF THE DEAR SAVIOR'S BIRTH! LONG LAY THE WORLD IN SIN AND ERROR..." He thought of lepers born on history's doorstep of the Christian church; how persons taunted them saying 'God is punishing you for your sin.' He thought how many gay persons with AIDS now had

110

to live like those lepers, living with the double stigma of being ostracized by society, and condemned by the religiously rigid present day standards. "...PINING, TILL HE APPEARED AND THE SOUL FELT ITS WORTH. A THRILL OF HOPE..." He envisioned gay persons who loved the church and who had been driven from it, one day returning as whole persons. "... THE WEARY WORLD REJOICES, FOR YONDER BREAKS A NEW AND GLORIOUS MORN!"

In the last verse his deep bass rattled, "CHAINS SHALL HE BREAK..." His voice cracked the 'k.' "... FOR THE SLAVE IS OUR BROTHER AND IN **HIS** NAME ALL OPPRESSION SHALL CEASE."

He was moving from the depths to climb the musical stairway to end the final chorus:

"O NIGHT WHEN CHRIST WAS BORN. O NIGHT DIVINE . . ."

Instead of holding the soaring note for the traditional three beats, he hung onto it acappella for a mind-stirring eleven full counts! This was his gift of encouragement for every struggling gay soul in God's present universe to hold on. When John paused for the breath that was to follow, it was as if the whole world stopped with him. In the stark silence one could only hear soft sniffling, revealing tears of touched lives in the now fully candle lit church. In his own quiet thoughts and to the congregation, he silently repeated the words of Jesus: "Do not weep for me. Weep for yourselves."

Then he ended: "O NIGHT, O NIGHT DIVINE!"

John slipped out of the pulpit stairwell leading

downstairs as the people began singing "Silent Night." He hung up his robe, put on his coat in the closet-like room where he warmed up, and left for the parking lot through an outside door from that tiny room. He wanted to avoid the accolades. It was misdirected praise.

As he drove down the freeway in his Jeep, his own eyes were now filled with water. White light from street lamps and oncoming cars refracted the tears in his eyes into a hundred fractured lightning bolts. When blinking red appeared in the corner of his right eye, he automatically pulled over to the side of the road.

Normally, nothing would make him stop. He quickly walked back to the lifeless car, and found an older lady sitting silently. The window was rolled down only an inch in the locked car. When he saw frightened eyes, and she saw tear filled eyes, both instinctively relaxed.

"It…it just stopped," she said.

John spoke up quietly, but immediately. "I'm John Davis," he began. I just finished singing at Evangelical Covenant Church for Christmas Eve. My parents are Ed and Gloria Davis. They live up on Hudson Drive." Then, thinking on his feet, he added, "My grandfather was Charlie Davis. He grew up in Wayland."

"The carpenter?" she responded immediately.

"Sure was," he returned, "The best!" "Look," John continued, "my Jeep's not as comfortable as your car, but it'll get us to a station."

She opened the door, and he carefully helped her to the Jeep.

She started by sharing that she was on her way home

from the Presbyterian Church service. Then she said, "My husband is home with a nurse attendant. I almost didn't go, but I don't get out much now, and I've never missed Christmas Eve. My name is Iris," she continued in the warmth of the car as they moved toward the freeway. "Iris Skinner. You can easily remember Iris. Just remember it's the flower with petals that open up to people; they reach down to the earth and up to God. That's what my mother and father told me all the time when I was growing up." Her voice fluttered with laughter as she said, "Yes, they did!"

The two hit it off like best friends from that instant, even though they were almost fifty years apart in age.

"You must have been an angel sent from God," Iris said slowly nodding her head. And then with sincere care added, "But angels don't usually have tear-filled red eyes."

In this cold, trouble stricken world, it was as if they were on their way to the Kingdom gates. John poured out to her what had happened the entire night, and when he finished he noticed tears in her eyes were brimming over onto her cheeks.

"I have a grandson who is gay," she said. "Even though his mother and I know about it, and we love him and he knows it, sometimes he's aloof, and sometimes he acts very uncomfortable around us. He never brings his friend home. I don't know whether it's him, or us, or both."

John shared and Iris listened. Iris shared and John listened. As the Jeep moved securely up the off ramp, Iris said with hesitation,

"I've always had a question."

"You can ask me anything," John returned, "I'll try my best to answer."

"Well, I...I just don't understand what you do," she started. "With my husband...I know all about that."

John gave a gentle smile, "Well, Iris, I guess I don't understand what you do either."

Iris smiled with a single chuckle, nodded her head once, and let the thought sink in.

John soon pulled the car into the well-lit station. The snow glistened all around them. The darkness had turned to dazzling white. As John turned to face Iris, her kindly face shone as she spoke with a depth of spirit: "You know that Bethlehem Inn? Well, there are a lot of Christians today still trying to stay with the innkeeper instead of staying out back with the Baby. They can't hear what you say. They just babble on. 'No room for you,' they keep saying. While the humble baby says to those who bend low to enter into His presence – from the poor shepherd to the wise rich sage, and that includes you and me, John, and all the others born like you and like me – 'Come on in. You *are* welcome *here*. Come on in and share the warmth.'"

John leaned over to give Iris a hug, and she kissed his cheek.

"I'll always be your friend," she continued. "I don't know where I'd be without you."

"That's a wonderful gift," John replied.

That Holy night as John stepped out into the snow of the station, he knew for himself the warmth known to each of those who had stepped inside the stable of Bethlehem.

*January 1, 1994*
*© Dr. Jerry Dickey*

"John and Iris's Holy Night"

# CHRISTMAS HUGS
# AND KISSES

*Story Nine*

$T$his will *not* be a Christmas to remember," Bill thought to himself as his new boots sloshed and crunched in the fresh snow. He hadn't worn boots since he was in grade school. Having been caught with only a pair of wing tips and a pair of penny-loafers, it was his only way to survive New York City's worst blizzard of the decade.

His two and a half days of business meetings for Amalgamated Steel couldn't have gone better. As vice-president of accounts, Bill knew the success of the past few days would not only keep his company's head above water next year, but also practically guarantee that it would reside in the black throughout the next year and a half. At the same time it was disheartening to discover that all the New York City airports were shut down because of the blizzard. His plane was supposed to have left two hours ago, and he should have been back in Ohio by now instead of plodding down 34th Street.

His wife Susan was one who faced life making something positive out of difficult situations, but he sensed her deflated body language even through the phone lines as he talked to her after the meeting ended.

"I'll go ahead with the kids to the shopping center this afternoon," Susi said trying to pick up her own spirits. "But it'll be so hard without you here for Christmas

Eve services tonight! We're all shoveled out here," she continued. "Chris and Kristi really went at it yesterday after school. Getting out at noon Friday gave them some sunshine to help warm them up in the ice and snow."

Warmth seemed to have been frozen out of the English language as Bill leaned into the grey swirling winds spitting stinging snow into his partially scarf-covered face. His Macy's shopping bag pelted his overcoat as it flapped like a seal trying to instigate audience applause. He had tried to turn his isolation into productivity. He had just finished going through Macy's picking up some specials on this last shopping day of Christmas, which the posters on the doors broadly proclaimed.

"I guess my chances of finding a second miracle on 34th Street in 1964 are about the same as getting hit twice by lightning," he mused to himself as he sloshed along.

Bill realized how hungry he was just as he saw the words, CITY DELI, lit up in neon. He stepped into the white tile entrance way, pushed open the white wood edged glass door, and felt instant relief from the hovering warmth of heated air. The small restaurant was jammed with local regulars, workers grabbing a quick cup of coffee as they headed home early, crazy shoppers devouring food for fuel, and a smattering of tourists like himself. On the right were three horseshoe counters with shiny white tops edged with ribbed silver. The right wall beyond the counters was filled with stainless steel stoves, refrigerators, coffee makers, and workspaces. The whole wall seemed to be huffing and puffing like a half-dozen Santas reveling in pipe smoke. The entire left wall of the small room was covered with a mirror. Along the bottom of the wall was a long expanse of cushioned brown vinyl benches behind a string of small tables. The patrons sat with their backs to the wall facing the aisle and the horseshoe counters. Bill saw one empty space in the whole restaurant along the left wall. A man's face with sky blue eyes and jet-black hair exchanged nonchalant glances as Bill moved toward the table next to him. Bill scooted in.

As Bill was removing his coat, scarf, and gloves, his mind told him he had made a mistake, an error in vision, a miscalculation. In the corner seat on his right had to be a child, not a man. Even at home in Columbus, Bill was not a person who would stare at others. He didn't intrude. He was thoughtful. He was respectful. But he had good peripheral vision. At six foot one, Bill towered above the table. The chin of this person was not much above table level.

Bill placed his coat on his left as the waitress came over to him.

"What can I getcha hon'?" she asked. Her bright red hair was a contrast to her black waitress uniform with its small white apron, white cuffed short sleeves, white handkerchief in the white edged pocket, and white, starched, tiara-like hat. Her black and white checkerboard nametag said, "Nora." Bill ordered steak and eggs, hash browns, toast, a tossed salad, apple pie, and coffee. He was starved.

Nora turned to the person on Bill's right, "Are you okay for now, Tony?" she questioned. The voice was not from a child. It resonated like the wind in an oil drum in the desert.

"I'm getting along just fine, Nora. Thanks for checking."

It was then Bill noticed in a side-glance that the man's arms stopped at the elbows, and somehow, in spite of that fact, he was eating toast and eggs and drinking coffee.

Everything seemed to fade away. The snow. The ice. The meetings. The family at home. The shopping. The fact that it was almost Christmas Eve. Voices were still murmuring throughout the restaurant while coffee pots were steaming and the food on the grill still sizzling. Bill's body was still thawing. But in his soul there was a deep quietness. During the passing moments in that little diner, he was almost in a hypnotic state. Bill was well aware that Tony was continuing to eat and was even more aware of his own confusion of how he managed it. Bill's own food had come and he began to eat.

Bill had seen that Tony had ham on his plate, and he thought it must be impossible for Tony to cut it with a knife and fork. He felt a kinship with this man sitting next to him. He certainly respected him. He would take no step to intrude.

The resonate, bass voice came again. This time it was directed toward Bill.

"Would you mind helping me out?" asked Tony.

As Bill turned to encounter Tony's full presence, the blue eyes were set in a face and head perfectly chiseled like one of those Roman marble busts from Italian museums he had visited while on summer trips when he was in college.

"Would you cut up my ham a little bit?" Tony began. "Nora's going non-stop today, so maybe you'd help."

"Sure," Bill said. As he scooted over to reach Tony's knife and fork, he realized Tony had a full torso, but his pants covered two short, rubbery legs that curled beneath him on the seat top where he sat. Bill cut the ham into small pieces. "Is this okay, Tony?" Bill asked.

"That'll work fine," Tony returned. "What's your name?" Tony continued.

"Bill. ...well, it's William, but I go by Bill."

"Well, mine is really Anthony Antonio Da Vinci Marioni," said Tony in his booming voice. "My parents wanted to give me a lot of choices," he chuckled. "You're not from New York are you?"

"No," said Bill with a gentle laugh, "Do I look that out of place?"

"I guess it was the scarf around your head and the boots," Tony replied with a wry smile as he easily maneuvered some ham to his mouth.

In that frozen world emerged a warm and caring conversation between two constellations traveling for a remarkable moment in the same orbit. How was it, in the midst of impossibilities that Christmas was, even today, reborn? When Bill was ready to leave, Tony asked him to take a card out of Tony's coat pocket.

"If you have time for a Christmas Eve service, we're easy to find!" Tony concluded, as they smiled their goodbyes.

On the subway trip back to his place, Bill was a solid mass of inner reflection. Three days ago, he had no idea what Christmas might become. His body swayed with the movement of the subway as Bill thought of the many people who wander through most of life searching and hoping for a place to give their gift. Today was one of God's most subtle miracles.

Before he knew it, Bill was off the subway, down the two silent blocks, and on the verge of entering his temporary shelter, a place named "The Admiral." It was a three-story "u" shaped apartment complex comprised of 32 executive apartment suites. At the open entrance to the courtyard were five Roman arches all lined in white lights. The walkway went through the center arch, and upon entering the courtyard one felt suspended amidst the surrounding heavenly light. The first and third stories had arched windows and all were outlined in white lights. The second floor windows were rectangles, and rather than being outlined in white lights, each window had an evergreen Christmas wreath glowing with studded white lights.

Bill took a deep breath as he stood in the inner courtyard. He sighed deeply as his mind reviewed the unusual events of this Christmas Eve day. Something in him had changed. Not with great fanfare like on the Damascus Road, or during a jolting earthquake, but something still, and small, and permanent deep within. His prayer became silence. His carol emerged as rising outgoing breaths of air. His spirit rose to the occasion as a receptive vessel for the blessings and work of the

Eternal God ever bending near earth's new born human life. The voice of the ages spoke silently as he looked back at the arch: "Enter God's gates with thanksgiving!"

Back in his apartment, Bill reached in his inner suit coat pocket and pulled out Tony's card. It read:

> You are cordially invited to attend
> Christmas Eve service
> with Tony and some of the heavenly host
> 7 PM
> Heavenly Host Methodist Church
> Theodore Parker Brown, D.D., minister

Bill looked at his watch. 5:17 PM. He felt his life was being guided like a detour from a freeway with an abundance of well-placed signs. In 45 minutes he had showered, freshened up, and added his red and blue striped tie to his dark blue suit. He made a few notations on the subway map, put on his boots, and he was off.

The IRT was still jammed with riders. The hum of the metal wheels on rails drowned out the last cold blasts of the blizzard now vacating the city for the frothy ocean water. It was only a block and a half walk to the quaint stone church from the subway stop.

His first instinct was to sit in the back row. But the red poinsettias surrounding the altar pulled him forward, and just as he was ready to turn to a pew half way down, he saw Tony in the front row. So he kept walking right on down the main aisle and turned to sit next to Tony. The organ music was quietly playing variations on "O Little

Town of Bethlehem." Tony flashed his warm smile. Bill instinctively put his hand on Tony's left shoulder, and Tony wrapped his upper arm around Bill's, and gave a pat to Bill's forearm.

Bill couldn't believe all that had happened today. But here on Christmas Eve he felt at home, and again a great sense of peace enveloped his whole being. Dr. Brown's prayer set a phrase forever in Bill's memory when he said, "The stranger in Bethlehem became the Christ child in order that the child in us could never be a stranger to God's children." Tony and Dr. Brown were equally as close as Bill's family, Susi, and Chris, and Kristi, in that moment of prayer.

As the service continued, the whole world past, present, and future seemed to fit together in Bill's mind. And the silence, the peaceful presence of physical silence surrounded all the spaces within the service that Christmas Eve. It may have been the harp music that added so much to the special moment, or it might have been the choir anthem in which 20 voices, only through humming, along with "ohs" and "ahs" and no words, somehow combined "Were You There?" with "Angels We Have Heard On High." It brought continuing goose bumps to Bill's neck and spine. But it was also the tearful impact of reading the sermon title in the bulletin: "God Always Has Room for One More."

After the final notes of the organ and harp postlude, Bill turned to thank Tony before he said goodbye. "I really don't have the words," he said, his voice choking a bit. Tony splashed his sparkling smile.

"God often arranges to get us right where we need to be," he returned.

Now Bill had always been a hand-shaker, not a hugger. But in the absence of a hand, he turned to Tony, bent over, and gave him a hug. He was somewhat startled to receive a kiss on his cheek in return. Bill was halfway up the aisle when he turned to see a whole line of people forming – men, women, and children waiting for their Christmas hugs and kisses from Tony.

Later that night, Bill stood again in the courtyard of The Admiral in New York City. In his mind's eye the two scenes merged: the lights outlining the apartment windows and entrance archways and the votive lights filling the communion railing at Tony's church, with the spotlighted giant wooden cross with the two quatrefoil circle designs on each side, and a field of giant, red poinsettias bathed in the same light of the cross. A thought jolted him. Bill suddenly realized that he had absolutely no idea how Tony got to and from either the deli or the church, not that it mattered how this happy person appeared like a miracle. But he didn't have a clue. Then Bill thought about the gift of God and the miracle of that arrival.

Bill went back to his room and called the front desk where the clerk was anxious to give him the news about flights, along with a message from Susi. He quickly called her back.

"Good news!" he began. "The front desk said the airlines added another flight to Columbus early tomorrow. So much happened tonight, Susi. Part of the heavenly host of Bethlehem is, of all places, right here in New York City! I can't wait to tell you all about it in person in a few hours."

Susi spoke up, "With all you've been through you'll probably just want to stay home tomorrow and have Christmas."

"Oh no, Susi," Bill said. "I'll be home in time for all of us to make it to the 10:45 AM church service. It's very important. You see, people will need some Christmas hugs and kisses. And you and Chris and Kristi and I can make a world of difference right there at home. I love you."

*February 14, 1995*
*© Dr. Jerry Dickey*

"Tony's Church"

# A CHILD OF CHRISTMAS

*Story Ten*

"Why do people have to die?" the eight year old said with deep wonderment.

As Jessie sat in the back seat looking out the window, she saw young joggers in sweats rhythmically pounding the sidewalks as their car moved up Randall Road away from the church. In her mind they transformed into the older women and men at the nursing home where her church choir sang yesterday. She had always contemplated life in ways far deeper than someone her age.

These young joggers with lithe strides and little body fat would grow older and die, in a short period of time, really. (In her mind's eye, they were doing that even now.) Nothing could stop that, she thought to herself. And her question continued to gather dimension as she thought, "Why all this effort just in order to die?"

A large, stately stone church tower stood across the street from the modern hospital. Its ancient tile roof hovered over the community like an English banker's umbrella. Its single giant bell struck the hours with a dull, deep voice sending out a seemingly unending tone. The reverberation moved like a lost echo traveling through a forest announcing that another tall tree had been felled.

As the bell struck two, icicles dropped clinking to the ground. They fell, shattering, as if trying to send their own message across the earth that no matter what was frozen on the surface of life, spring was already beginning. For whether we are ready or not, new life is excitedly gathering steam beneath the earth to break forth at the appointed time.

No one knows the appointed hour for life or death. But Christmas touches our struggling earth each year in unexpected places, which God creates for us. And so it was to be. Through the centuries, from the very birth of Christ onward, the child HAS entered into the gift of life, but not without struggle and not before buffeting the obstacles of the day.

Jessie met her day's challenges one after the other. She may have been a child, but she had the stubborn, determined tenacity contributed by her grandmother's DNA. Today it was released with full force.

First, she had to cross the somewhat slippery sidewalk outside the hospital in her black patent leather shoes which she had worn especially for her grandmother. They were her grandmother's Christmas present the year before. She made her way carefully while carrying her guitar. Her aunt, who was with her, had suggested more practical boots before Jessie left home.

"Even if Grandma doesn't see them today," Jessie replied, "someday she'll know I wore the shoes she gave me. Besides, God knows," she added, "and that's certainly worth the effort!"

She already looked like a miracle as she leaned into the wind. She conquered the parking lot with the neck of her guitar case pointed forward like the bow of an Arctic icebreaker ship.

The hospital sounds and smells were predictable, while interrupted by perfumes, kitchen aromas woven into fabrics, and the tobacco smell of an overcoat plucked from the hall tree in a household of smokers.

Jessie was surprised to find that no one entered a room without scrubbing up, and putting on appropriate attire. They were led to a small prep room where she washed her hands vigorously. She put her arms through the yellow hospital gown and folded the one-size-fits-all gown a few times around the waist until her shiny shoes showed at the bottom. Then she tied the waist strings snugly. Next, she fastidiously tied the facemask over her nose and mouth and her neatly combed hair. Finally she donned those annoying, stretchy, latex gloves.

Jessie and her aunt stood at the entrance to hospital room 2867. Her aunt partially pulled back the privacy curtain located a few steps beyond the doorway and the two of them entered the room.

A string of bells hung from the silver sidebars pulled up to keep Grandmother Susie safely in bed. Next to them hung a grey rectangular radio monitor with red and green rectangular buttons. Next to that was a tan square bed control monitor with four buttons to adjust the bed.

Susie's daughter rang the bells softly. They had a gentle angelic tone. A preacher had sent them from Ohio. For more than thirty years he had been included in Susie's family, ever since his first appointment following seminary at the church where Susie had been a secretary. Some family and friends had called her Susie Belle.

Because of that, over the years the preacher had often sent her bells for Christmas. This Christmas had been no exception. Two weeks ago, he had sent them to the hospital in Texas.

Susie opened one eye. She offered a closed smile as she rocked her head back and forth on the pillow.

"I love you, Mom," her daughter returned. "And Jessie loves you too. Do you remember what day it is today? It's Christmas day, and Jessie made the hour-long drive with me this morning to bring you a special present.

Susie licked her lower lip, rested a minute, and then opened both eyes. She looked at the ceiling, then at her daughter, and then turned her head so that her cheek was on the pillow as her eyes searched for her granddaughter.

"Jessie's right here," Susie's daughter said. "She wrote a new Christmas song just for you," she continued with the distinct diction of a seasoned teacher. She moved to the side of the room, and sat on the sofa over which hung a picture of Rothenburg ob der Tauber, a historic town on southern Germany's Romantic Road.

Jessie moved up to the sidebars of the bed and looked deep into Susie's eyes with a love that was so elemental and permanent that it overwhelmed the room. She was here to do battle with the pain and debilitation of two major heart operations over the past eight months, and three life-threatening strokes of the past three days. They were to be no match for this young girl's presence.

Jessie had titled Susie's song, "CHRISTMAS BRINGS FAMILY TOGETHER." She began. The hospital mask muted the clear, beautiful voice.

"CHRISTMAS BRINGS FAMILY
TOGETHER
THROUGH ICE AND WINTER
WEATHER..."

A doctor, a nurse, and a preacher had moved into the entranceway. Abruptly, they stopped at the partially opened curtain. The nurse's hands were cupped over the forearms of the doctor and the preacher as one holds the steel walkway bars for support in the rehabilitation unit downstairs. These modern sages were witnesses to God's incarnation and Emmanuel. Transfixed, they stood silent throughout the song.

"...AND THAT WILL ALWAYS BE
SINCE YOU BECAME CHRISTMAS
TO ME..."

Jessie had spent a long time thinking of just the right words to help her grandmother get better.

"...LOVE IS THE BEST GIFT
THAT CHRISTMAS CAN BRING..."

Her fingers hit their mark on the guitar neck, in spite of the rubber glove tips dangling from the ends of her fingers. It was an Olympic performance.

"...LOVE IS THE BEST GIFT
THAT'S WHY MY HEART CAN SING..."

Yesterday, Jessie had looked at the pictures in her Christmas album. One section held the "With love from Susie Belle" tags from all the presents she had been given over the years.

"...DEAR, DEAR MERRY
CHRISTMAS
TO YOU THIS DAY..."

The guitar sounds hovered over the hospital room like the angel voices over the Bethlehem hillsides.

"...WE'RE GOING TO WALK
TOGETHER A LONG, LONG WAY!"

It was one of those moments hospital efficiency couldn't have arranged. The grace of God had gathered lives together like the stitches of an heirloom quilt bringing warmth to this Christmas rebirth. It bound unrelated hearts together forever.

When Jessie finished, she put the guitar down. Then she stood tall, and reached through the silver sidebars. Her grandmother's wrists were tied to them to keep her from pulling the tubes from her throat. Jessie saw the red marks from her attempts. She took her grandmother's hand in her glove-covered hands and gave it a squeeze. Jessie noticed each finger. In spite of the body's struggle, Susie's hand still curved nimbly with beautiful nails. The hands that had served others so faithfully over a lifetime – making pots of homemade vegetable soup for youth groups, adroitly writing columns of figures for income tax forms capably and faithfully filed for countless family members and friends. These hands now waited for the care of others. And, it was *that* care she needed. It would strengthen her own will so that she could return to the world she had loved and served so dutifully for decades. Jessie felt a faint squeeze come in response, which suddenly became amazingly strong.

Jessie's left hand moved to the silver bells hanging on the bedside railing. She rang the bells. Their soft shimmering sounds echoed across their joined right hands. A tear of joy rolled down Susie's right cheek. Their eyes were locked in a twinkle. Just then, Susie's eyes began to lose that hollow, haunted look of isolated fear. It was at that moment that both Jessie and Susie knew they were going to be around for many more Christmases. And they were. And you and I know why.

*Please know that any year you choose to give a Christmas bell, you may be giving another Christmas miracle. Remember that when the joyous angel voices quieted on the hillsides of Bethlehem, a tiny bell was heard. It was that tiny sheep bell that carried the music through the winding, sleepy pathways of Bethlehem right up to the cradled cry of God, gently opening the eyes of our waiting, ever-weary world.*

*Jessie's music, nestled among the gently ringing bells, is just the most recent in a long line of carols bringing peace on earth, good will to men, women, children, as well as a doctor, a nurse, and a preacher.*

*But this is exactly how the graceful gifts of God multiply.*

*It was Jessie's song, which became the foundation for three new Christmas stories in the lives of three unsuspecting witnesses. But those are other stories. This day there is but one thought you need to remember: If your heart is focused on love, YOU may have a hand in God's next Christmas miracle! And you may help Christmas bells ring during someone else's dear, dear Merry Christmas.*

*October 1998 through
September 2000
© Dr. Jerry Dickey*

"Bells for Grandmother Susie"

# CHRISTMAS FAR FROM HOME

## Story Eleven

If truth is better than fiction, then my journey of Christmas 1967 is a classic. For much of my life I had dreamed about being an exchange student so I could travel to some enchanting country far away from home and enjoy life from a different perspective than the one I had known. But exchange students needed top grades to be chosen, and it would be 30 years before I achieved that. Perhaps traveling was in my DNA. As an adult I learned that my mother had wanted to be a missionary, but chose to get married and raise three children instead.

Perhaps some ancestor of hers had been a navigator on a seafaring vessel traveling the great oceans. Perhaps someone early in her lineage traveled the ancient spice road to China, or studied elephants in Africa, or traversed frozen highways over the Alps. Who knows if one forbearer of the earliest days might even have been a wise sage from the East who followed a new unknown star into the heart of history's manger? For there within the heartbeat of the timeless hope of that first Christmas, strangers in a cold, forgotten world brought and received the gift of welcome.

On Saturday, July 1, 1967, I left New York City for an eleven-month stay in Europe. During the months before, I had communicated with embassies and cultural exchange centers of European countries. I gathered the pamphlets and brochures they sent which I then pored over. Finally, out of the stacks of possibilities, I created a year of study, living, and travel on a budget that would make a person today pause with wonderment. Round trip air fare, six schools and study opportunities in Denmark, Germany, and France; 15,000 miles of train travel through 13 countries in that first summer alone, plus the added blessing of walks and talks with persons literally from every corner of God's world. All this on a "shoestring" budget of $2,400.

I wrote a detailed daily journal that year – a task I have never achieved since. Even today, I can vividly relive thoughts and feelings and attitudes that I had morning, noon, and night about daily life. I remember well the feeling I had the day I boarded an Aer Lingus jet for Ireland and then Europe. I thought to myself that when I returned a year later it would seem but as a day. And so it did. Just as life itself seems but a day whenever the sun finally sets.

And somewhere in the midst of struggle and contentment, joy and sorrow, belief and doubt, work and prayer – is Christmas. Christmas rises from the landscaped plateau of life – evergreen in hope, scented in renewal, just when our lives are pining, lifting branches of light to every corner of earth's darkness. It is a gift from God. It is the ever-renewing Christ event called Christmas.

It was a meaningful journey as I made my way as a stranger throughout Europe day by day. Like each of you, I have been on the receiving end of life since it began

– parents, grandparents, brothers, sisters, uncles, aunts, cousins, as well as friends and their extended families fed us, provided for us, taught us, loved and cared for us. Did we earn that care? Did we pay for it? Did we deserve it? It is that gift of love that gives us life.

When one becomes a stranger wandering in a foreign land, this gift is all the more life changing as one is welcomed, fed, given shelter, met and sent off at train stations, by persons one chances to meet.

On July 28th, I left Venice for Munich, where I paid my tuition of $315 for the fall term at the Goethe Institut which was to last from October 26th to December 22nd. On July 29th, I was on a train again headed north through Germany to Odense, Denmark, and with little sleep, made my way onward to Svenborg and Ollerup, the tiny village no one back in Ohio could find for me on maps of Denmark.

My destination was the eight-day Danish Gymnastic College summer course in Ollerup. There for the first time in my life, I was the foreigner, one of 75 from around the world settling in among 200 Scandinavian students. The eight-day course was packed with mornings of theory class and practical gymnastics. Afternoons were filled with three hours of gymnastics and swimming. After only one day I wrote, "Talk about tired? I was dead." Five meals a day and constant movement helped to dissipate sore muscles, stiff neck, sprains, and bruises.

But think about it. The wise sages who journeyed to Bethlehem had more to deal with than saddle sores. And consider the shepherds: keeping sheep safe in starlight, without stepping in a hole or tripping over some ancient stone, certainly was no easy task. My trip was like the ancient journey to Bethlehem, where travelers who were far from home had no place to stay.

Poul Erik Thomsen was his name. God plunked him down next to me at breakfast that Saturday morning at the Gymnastic College the day before departure. He said he was moved by my spoken thoughts before I sang "Born Free" at the International talent show the night before. When he heard of my travels, he asked me if I would visit Aalborg, Denmark, where he was a teacher, and teach a few of his classes. Having shared that he was in the summer session for soccer and physical education teachers, and not the gymnastics course I was in, I replied, "I'd be happy to visit and help you teach, as long as it doesn't include soccer!"

"We could just stay with (pause) English," he said with a straight face and dry humor, which from that time on he always knew would trip my face up with a smile.

Poul Erik's wife's name was Inger Margarethe, but everyone called her Søster – which meant sister. Together they would become a gift of Christmas I would never forget.

I attended the University of Copenhagen in August following the gymnastic summer course. I traveled. I taught Poul Erik's classes. At the Goethe Institut, where I enrolled to study the German language in Rothenburg ob der Tauber, I saw leaves turn from green to gold, orange, and red. Finally the leaves drifted earthward leaving branches blanketed with wet snow turning my world into a silent, lofty cathedral. That was my life from October 28th to December 22nd.

In school, Richard Raymond Albert Bruggemann was my best friend. I was in the beginning German class. He was in the advanced. Though he was ten years my junior, I delighted in telling others that he was my twin brother. He got an even bigger kick telling people that it was true. Rick had a car. Marie Noelle Marquis, from Paris, was with us so often on trips we became the three musketeers on wheels.

Rick's father was half Japanese and half German. His mother was Spanish. Rick grew up in Japan, would later marry a Norwegian, and have three towheaded kids that would turn heads as they paraded along with their parents down their hometown streets of Kobe, Osaka, and Tottori.

Rick, the organized business manager type, had made arrangements for me to spend Christmas with his grandparents in northern Germany near Warstein. On Thursday, December 21st, he found out one of them was sick, and it was going to be impossible for me to spend Christmas there. Mentally floundering, I felt the squeeze of the unknown. That week I had received two letters that were to re-create Christmas from scratch. One was from Poul Erik which said he had supposed I might spend part of Christmas with them in Aalborg. The other was from Mikael Poulson, also living in Aalborg, Denmark, who had been in the student hostel where I had stayed when I was in Italy the previous summer.

I decided to go as far north as I could by car with

Rick on December 22$^{nd}$, and then take the train to Denmark. Poul Erik had no telephone, but during the five hour drive north, I remembered I had Mikael Poulsen's number, so we stopped at a post office which is where one made phone calls in those days. I called. Mikael's mother answered. She knew me right away, even though I only talked to her once before for a few seconds. I had never met any other members of Mikael's family.

"Yes, Jerry," she began, "did you get Mik's letter before you left? Good, he was afraid you might not. Can't stay in Germany for Christmas? Well, just come on up and stay here with us. Your friends are here? Yes. And you want them to know you'll be here on Sunday? Could you spell the name? Good, and I'll have Mikael get in touch with Erik. He'll be home at eight. And we'll look forward to seeing you this time too! Have a safe trip. It's a little foggy here. We'll see you soon. Goodbye."

On Friday, December 22$^{nd}$, Rick and I arrived at Warstein, Germany, and found that I could get an overnight train leaving at 8:15pm and with changes would arrive in Aalborg by 4:05pm Saturday the 23$^{rd}$. I had told Mrs. Poulsen I would arrive Sunday, but decided to forge ahead. The trains were packed. I endured one four-hour stopover and the changes were hectic. A 60-year old German lady found out about a change I had to make I didn't even know about, and sent me scurrying off the train with apples and some of her homemade cookies. "Alles gute," she waved. "All the best."

Tired, but hopeful, I arrived in Aalborg, Denmark. I got a cab for the four-kilometer ride to Poul Erik and

Søster's. Under grey skies, the taxi drove up the black pavement to the left of the long three-story apartment building. It had walkway balconies across the front of the flat grey cement building. The building had yellow brick sides with stairwells at each end. As we pulled up, Poul Erik, Søster, and their new, as yet unnamed 11-day old daughter "Little Søster" were just that minute arriving home.

I look back on those moments now with the same wonderment with which shepherds stood transfixed with angelic voices filling dark Bethlehem skies. For my life, that moment was the "fullness of time" written about in scripture. You see, I had no Danish money. Poul Erik and Søster had not been home, and had not yet received the message from Mikael.

Poul Erik gave me some Danish money to pay for the cab. They ushered me, along with their child of Christmas, into the four-room apartment. Some walls were light blue, others white. In the living room at the back of the apartment stood the Danish Christmas tree with candles waiting to be lit.

The Christmas tree, some say, began in Germany with Martin Luther who brought a tree indoors for the first time. In Denmark, the tradition was to celebrate Christmas with a real tree brought indoors, with real candles added. The small candles were placed in weighted holders that kept them right side up. They were lit only on Christmas Eve or Christmas Day while family circled the tree holding hands as they sang Danish carols. That moment was always the highlight of a Danish Christmas, then the candles were promptly extinguished. Once I understood the care taken with fire on live trees, this safety-conscious American could be enthralled.

During my Christmas week in Aalborg, I stayed with both families. Christmas Eve I was with Poul Erik, Søster, Little Søster, Søster's parents, and her younger brother, Søren. Dinner included duck, pork, vegetables and a rice pudding desert with one nut hidden in it – the one who found it in their dessert got a present. Later, the candles on the tree were lit and the six of us held hands and sang carols as we walked around the tree. As we sang, red hearts, used in decorating for a Danish Christmas, spun lazily over the dining table. I still have the two presents I received: a paper bound book from Poul Erik and Søster and four handkerchiefs wrapped as paper cigars from Søster's brother, Søren. On Christmas Eve it snowed and on Christmas Day everything was blanketed with snow.

On Christmas Day, I was with the Poulsens. Mikael's grandparents had made reservations for ten of us at the Hotel Phoenix for dinner, and I joined my second Danish family. The next few nights I was back at Poul Erik's. Three and a half decades later, Søster would remind me that as soon as I arrived at the apartment door I asked, "Do you have any rice pudding left I can have?"

I can't tell you what would have happened if the five hour journey to northern Germany hadn't given me time to think, and remember where to find Mikael Poulsen's phone number, or if Mrs. Poulsen hadn't answered the phone as if she were just waiting to invite me home, or if Poul Erik and Søster hadn't just returned home right before I arrived with no Danish money to pay the cab driver, or if the Danish Christmas tree hadn't permanently illuminated itself into my heart and memory to be re-kindled into your Christmas this year.

But it did. And today the Danish Christmas tree rises in my memory from the fallen needles of long ago, with renewed light. Let it remind us that the darkness of the unknown has never overcome the light, and that it never will. The light is for living. Those who have gone before us will never die. Only a child can bring that hope; only the Christ can lead us home.

Following the hope of a star, they came from afar. And in that field there were shepherds watching over their flock. O Christmas tree, O Christmas tree. Evergreen, ever seen. You lift our eyes with light from earth to heaven.

"Have a safe trip. It's a little foggy here. We'll see you soon."

And somewhere across the lands, two days before Christmas, one is accepted and expected, and no one living should have to search for more than that for Christmas. That itself IS Christmas!

*December 8, 2002*
*© Dr. Jerry Dickey*

*Left to right:* Søster Thomsen, Poul Erik Thomsen
*Photo taken by* Jerry Dickey, Summer of 1967

*Left to right:* Dr. Jerry Dickey, Lotte Thomsen,
Jakob Lindahl
*Photo taken by* Dr. Will Cann, Spring of 2002

# THE RENEWABLE LIGHT OF CHRISTMAS

## Story Twelve

It was the last hurrah – a combination of Bethlehem, the silver lining of eternity, and the return of Jesus Christ himself. It was Christmas, and no one in Jerry's congregation would ever forget it.

Everyone is searching for the light, for warmth and care in an unfriendly world. It happened in Bethlehem. It happened in Gethsemane's garden. It happened in Eden, in Ephesus, and in epiphanies throughout the ages. And I guarantee it's going to happen to you. Not when you plan it, but when God decides you need it.

Now mind you, David Leroy Climer, who chose to go by the name Jerry, would not live long enough to see the intersections of Christmas traditions that year, but he would be responsible for giving them life.

"Jerry the Preacher," as Anna and Ella and others in his prayer power and lay ministry training groups re-nicknamed him, would leave a legacy that would last long beyond his days. Anna Brown McCandless was to work this miracle at the age of 75, and in the final process, she would shake up the conditioned minds and hearts of her people at church like a minor earthquake.

On the first weekend in December, Jerry's wife Joyce took their children to see their grandparents in Boston, where Joyce could enjoy a rare four-day respite from her busy nursing career. Jerry had accepted an invitation to be part of Ella's extended family at their country club Christmas party on that Sunday. Anna was invited too. She drove to the parsonage, and from there Jerry and Anna went together to the party.

They arrived 15 minutes early. Anna, resembling the twelve-year old Jesus with the Temple rabbis, conversed with strangers and asked questions at the hors d'oeuvres table in the center of the room. When Ella arrived in a sleek holiday sweater and black skirt, she greeted Jerry and Anna and the three of them passed time talking about family, political issues, preacher's sermons, and Jerry's insistence that one of them should change seats with him so he didn't have to face the women's restroom door opening and closing. After a Christmas dinner buffet, all were called to gather in the Great Room for carols and the arrival of Santa.

That's when it came out. As long and as well as Jerry the Preacher had known Anna, he had no idea how disconcerting the idea of Santa Claus was to her.

"I'd like to kick him up the down escalator!" she began.

Jerry was no ardent promoter of the jolly elf, but in this case, he moved to Santa's defense. He told Anna a story of Doug Adams, a professor of his at seminary, who taught a course called "Biblical Humor."

"If you're dead serious about your faith, allowing no room for humor," Doug was known to repeat, "your faith is dead." Doug was so animated that laughter often filled their classroom.

In class, Doug held up an Advent/Christmas stole

done in beautiful purples and blues, which his wife, Margo, had made for a doctoral student. "This," he said with a grin as he turned it over, "is for the preacher who really gets upset when people bring Santa into Christmas." On the reverse side, the stole was stitched with rollicking Santas in bright red, white, and green!

Before leaving the party, Jerry gave Ella a holographic Sunflower sack with Christmas presents wrapped in gold and white. He had tried to finish Anna's present too, but at 2 am the night before, he had fallen asleep.

After the party, Anna dropped Jerry at home where he fell asleep on the bed, fully dressed, with lights burning in four rooms. At 4 am he awoke, and finished wrapping Anna's presents along with those for other church stalwarts – Carolyn, Jim and Sue, and Les and Jane. Presents, he would happily remind his friends, were part of his calling!

Monday night, December 2nd, he phoned Anna at 7 pm but no one answered.

"This is Santa," he said into her answering machine, "I have your presents." At 9:30 he called again. When Anna answered, she said she hadn't heard the phone because she was out of the room and didn't think of checking her messages because her Monday night football game was on and that *always* took precedence over everything else.

"I'm coming over with your presents!" Jerry exclaimed.

"Oh, why don't you wait 'til I can pick them up," she pleaded, "and just save yourself the drive?"

"Nope, things are going to get hectic from here on,

and you need to have this beautiful sack of presents to look at for 21 days, so you can get excited about what's in them!" he replied.

On the drive over, Jerry's mind contemplated anew Jesus' birth, the issues of starlight, his Advent sermons, and Santa. Throughout life, Jerry had seen scenes of Jesus' birth in the manger portrayed mostly by children and youth, but never by a cast of older adults. Throughout the ages crèche scenes evolved, both artistically and through their human portrayal.

The Christian Saint Nicholas had evolved in medieval Europe, to become Jolly Old St. Nicholas, and finally the Santa Claus of the 21st century. On dark curvy roads that evening, he passed objects that lit up and sent a glow across a lawn or a street: a snowman, a sparkling evergreen tree, a manger, then a Santa face. Each light brought a smile to his face. He thought to himself how encouraging it was to see ANY kind of light on such a pitch-black night. Anna was going to get a sermon.

"Anna," he said with a grin, "I've been thinking all the way over here!" The feisty little lady remained silent. She knew he was on his soapbox, and nothing she could do would stop the sermon. "I've been up two late nights wrapping presents. Then, at 9:30 at night, I'm driving an hour across town and back so you can have a star-studded bag of gifts to wonder about during these long nights leading up to Christmas. Now tell me you don't believe in Santa Claus!"

"I believe you're Santa Claus," she said cautiously,

knowing full well she herself would bring the sermon to yet a higher level!

"No, Anna," he said. "We are all Santas. We are all Bethlehem angels. We are all the Christ child. Saint Paul himself said, 'For me to live *is* Christ.' In a dark world, you and I become the gift: the love of God, a light, a surprise of hope, a present in the present, a gift of child breathed into the aging, weary, hassled, confused, embattled world of every today!"

Jerry smiled. Along with a Christmas bag imprinted with gold stars and brimming with gifts, he handed Anna a 3 by 5 inch piece of goldenrod paper with a fish symbol and Lay Ministry Training printed across the top. Her year of classes had finished last spring. She recognized her own handwriting on the piece of notepaper. At the last session, the class had been told to write what ministries each one would like to be involved in at church. Above her signature Anna had written, "Anything but being creative."

"Anna," Jerry said with a smile, "in two weeks time, you and I are going to create a live Christmas card manger scene that will knock everyone's socks off! The characters at the manger are going to be your age." With hardly a pause, he added, "If Sarah can have a baby at 90, you can certainly stand by a manger at 75 as Mary!" He gave Anna a hug, and he was gone.

*Tuesday morning, December 3rd, 9 am:* Anna's phone rang. It was Ella.

"Anna, Jerry's gone."

"Gone where?" replied Anna.

165

"Joyce took the kids to school from the airport this morning," Ella continued. "She went to the church office, and was following him home in separate cars. I don't know. His car went off the road and hit a tree. Joyce cradled him in her arms. He's gone."

Anna sat, immobile and mute. A page had turned. Jerry the Preacher was gone. Anna couldn't see or feel anything. She couldn't think. She just sat.

At 11 am her phone rang again. It was Jerry's wife, Joyce. "Anna, I have a preacher for Sunday, December 7th." Her voice was willful and strong. "Will you please do the service on the 14th? When Jerry got home last night, he called us in Boston and told me that he talked to you about doing something special."

Anna blinked back the tears. "I don't know how," she said, "I don't know how, but I will...yes...I will."

"Oh, and Anna, Jerry built the stable backdrop last week," said Joyce. "It's in the garage. The secretary has Brian's number from our former church. He's been thinking about a star. I love you, Anna," she concluded.

"I love you, Joyce."

Anna sat stunned for another 15 minutes amid tears and fears. Then her eyes settled on her Quaker grandmother's rocking chair in the corner. In the blink of an eye, the back seat of her car was down, and the rocking chair was in the trunk. By noon she was sitting in front of the altar in that very same rocking chair. Every day, Anna sat rocking from 12 noon until 2 pm with her Bible, a pencil and paper, and her silent prayers. Every hour before and after, her work ethic was unstoppable.

In the quiet church, she heard the on and off hum of traffic. An ambulance siren pierced the afternoon at one point. She heard an airplane engine overhead approach and disappear. Her thoughts vacillated from peace to resignation to anger then to frustration. She kept on rocking.

That is where her vision unfolded. She was determined to give a rebirth to Christmas like no one had ever imagined. The characters portraying the first Bethlehem Christmas were to be retired, active saints of faith. She called her Jewish friend, Steve.

"Stephen," she began, "Jerry the Preacher said in class that his Old Testament professor, Dr. Beck, told him, 'You can't be a good Christian, until you're a good Jew.' I need your help."

"Anna," Steve said, "I don't know what kind of a mission you're on now, but I've known you long enough to know you're determined; how can I help?"

Then she called Shubha.

"I know you're involved with your family and grandchildren here, and you phone your relatives in India every week, so if anyone can be a wise sage from the East traveling to Bethlehem, it's you. You have more credentials than all of us. The gift you'll carry will be a green and yellow lotus blossom – it'll be the eastern version of the evergreen Christmas tree. And it'll light up," she added. That thought broke through to her mind right then, while on the telephone, like sunlight through a winter cloud.

Two days passed. Anna again sat in the rocking

chair in front of the altar looking at the cross. She felt the presence of Jerry, who would have started his 34th year of life the following week. A sentence sealed itself in her mind: Through the suffering of the world shines the light of God's love.

There before the altar of God she decided that there would be one exception to her casting of older adults. His name was Todd S. Dutton, the nephew of her best friend, Julie Beeson. He was 37, and along with child-onset diabetes, he was HIV-positive. She had not seen him for seven months. She dialed his number.

"Todd, this is Anna. I'm sorry I haven't kept in touch, and as of today that's changing. What's your favorite pie? I know it needs to be sugar free. Okay, you got it. I'll be over in four hours. Bye."

She arrived at his doorstep with a sugarless version of peanut butter pie that was straight from heaven.

"I need your help at church," she began.

Todd countered, "I haven't been in a church for twenty years!"

"And for good reason," Anna came back quickly, "but I'm here to make up for that! Life is too short, and love is too lacking. I need you to go shopping with me tomorrow to get some material, and to help me create some costuming and lighting. What clothes do you regularly wear?"

Todd responded, "Mostly black – t-shirts and Levis."

"That'll work great," she replied. "And I want you to be a king." she added.

"I'm more comfortable being a Queen!" he returned, grinning widely.

Anna stood on her toes and stretched her hands to the neck of his 6' 2" strong racing bike frame. "We all have to branch out!" she said wryly, as she gave him a hug. "I'll pick you up tomorrow at 2:30 pm sharp." A year and a half later she would be in the front row for Todd's funeral.

That night, at home, she made a long distance call to Brian. "Brian, this is Jerry-the-Preacher's Anna calling. It's a difficult time, so we need a very special star. I don't know how, but it has to be a star of Bethlehem like no one has ever created before, and I know it's not an easy task."

"Well, Anna," Brian returned, "if it were easy, you could walk down the street and ask anyone to do it! You'll have your star. And Anna, you and I know Jerry won't be there. But you and I also know, he will."

"Thank you, Brian," she said as she sniffled, through tears. "We're working at light from the inside out now," she said. "Part of the outside light is gone. Oh, Brian," she added, "we also need three gifts that symbolically light up from the inside, and a couple of lights for Joseph and the shepherd!"

"That'll be easy," he returned. Brian heard Anna's sigh of relief, a hundred miles away over the phone.

The first weekend arrived. Yes, they went to Jerry's funeral and, yes, they were flooded with tears, but they were too busy living the legacy to collapse or be stopped in their tracks.

Anna was back in her grandmother's rocking chair. Ella would be the angel. Two other retired persons would help, one as Joseph, and the other as a hillside shepherd. She decided each performer would carry a light except her character, Mary. The lights of those helping her would be the only light she needed.

It was Sunday, December 14th. The community of faith, though battered by life, had gathered together in large numbers.

How can I help you to see and to feel that moment?

As the people arrived, Anna was seated in her rocking chair in front of the altar. During the liturgical part of the service, she moved to the front pew with Ella. When it was time for the offering, all were startled and wide-eyed, for following after the ushers, Santa came down the aisle with a giant sack filled to the brim! While the people gave their tithes and offerings, Santa gave each one a present with a star on it to take home with them, a reminder of the renewable light of Christmas. It was at that moment Anna felt Jerry's presence, and his parting hug at her home, less than two weeks before.

While the scripture was read, she gathered the senior citizens, and young Todd, and with silent gestures, sent them off to their places.

Anna moved past her grandmother's rocking chair to the pulpit. She didn't enter the pulpit, but stood next to it and rested her right hand on the wood rail. With her left hand, she held a paper, which had words she had carefully crafted from her rocking chair. Her sweater had white stars with pearls on them.

She began to read:

"The light is for everyone. Our beloved pastor, David Leroy Climer – Jerry the Preacher – already knew that. So many of us left behind here still have to learn it. The light is for *everyone*! In our most honest moments, each of us knows that. It is in the push and shove of this world that we learn to deny it." Anna repeated it a third time, very slowly: "The...light...is...for...every...one." She continued, "No creed or custom, no lessons or liturgy, no majority vote or membership certificate outshines this renewable light given to all of us by God. If you do not give your life for this light of truth, then you will end up giving it for a lot of lesser lights." Anna ended, "I want to thank the world. For the persons helping me today represent more of God's diverse world than most churches care to welcome or include. Pray for this amazing, renewable light. We will need it, more than anything else, for the journey before us."

With different music for each one entering, the elderly cast portraying the first Christmas moved from different parts of the darkened sanctuary carrying lamps and gifts that shone in a variety of colored light. When all had gathered in front of Jerry the Preacher's beautiful stable backdrop, they lifted their lights as one. Santa then entered from the door behind the pulpit, walked to Anna's rocking chair in front of the altar, and with a gentle look at the elderly persons in the crèche scene, and a smiling nod to the congregation, turned and sat in Anna's chair facing the altar, and rocked.

Then Brian's star, like a halo over history, emerged

from the darkness and cast rays of light like remnants from the Big Boom, shimmering over the manger into the congregation. As drops of water that evaporate and return to the earth, constantly renewed, those sparkling beams of light from that star became a permanent, transforming reminder of the love of God in the hearts, minds, and souls of that congregation. It was captivating. The silent light of "Silent Night" became theirs.

"And now the light is yours," Anna said softly. "The beams of that Bethlehem star are a renewable gift of light directly from God, through David Leroy "Jerry" Climer, to me, Anna Brown McCandless, and now, to you. It's your light to give away for all eternity."

As the music continued, the sanctuary became once more the sanctuary Anna had known, while rocking in front of the altar during the past two weeks. It was the cradle of the light of the living God, of the eternal now and forever.

*December 30, 2002;*
*September 30, 2003*
*© Dr. Jerry Dickey*

"Friends Create Christmas"

Father, that Thy love may be known, open our hearts; that Thy truth may be known, open our minds; that Thy spirit may be known, open our souls; and grant, O God, in that openness, that we may learn to live the abundant life in Jesus' name. Amen.

*Written by Jerry Dickey, 1964*
*The original lithograph artwork was a gift to him*
*by Simon C. Nielsen, Jr.*

May the light of the Christ Child
fill **your** journey with hope
and welcome you home.

Printed in the United States
By Bookmasters